Ed knew s[...]

All her mone[...] [...]o
sell if someo[...] [...]e
buying it—as [...] have done.

"We need to start with the foundation and wiring first," Ed offered when he saw that she was speechless.

"Look, Ed," Jill finally said. "I know all the dinners I can cook for you and your friends won't be enough to pay for the work this place needs." Glancing around frantically, she said, "I'll pay you a little bit each month until it's paid off."

He didn't want to take money from her, but he wasn't about to take away every last shred of her pride either. Nodding slowly, he replied, "Okay, it's a deal, but only for the materials. We'll exchange labor for dinners."

"Keep track of everything," she said as she looked directly at him with her big brown eyes that sent his heart into overdrive.

"You bet I will."

And he meant it, too. He would keep track of absolutely everything—from her soulful eyes, her creamy skin, her hair that was in desperate need of brushing, all the way to her pink-painted toenails that peeked out from her sturdy sandals.

DEBBY MAYNE has been a freelance writer all her adult life, starting with slice-of-life stories in small newspapers, then moving on to parenting articles for regional publications and fiction stories for women and girls. She has been involved in all aspects of publishing—from the creative side, to editing a national health magazine, to freelance proofreading for several book publishers. Her belief that all blessings come from the Lord has given her great comfort during trying times and gratitude for when she is rewarded for her efforts. She has a charming husband, two beautiful grown daughters, a super sweet son-in-law, and two very spoiled cats.

Books by Debby Mayne

HEARTSONG PRESENTS
HP625—Love's Image

Double Blessing

Debby Mayne

Heartsong Presents

A note from the Author:
I love to hear from my readers! You may correspond with me by writing:

Debby Mayne
Author Relations
PO Box 721
Uhrichsville, OH 44683

ISBN 978-1-59789-623-8

DOUBLE BLESSING

Our mission is to publish and distribute inspirational products offering exceptional value and biblical encouragement to the masses.

PRINTED IN THE U.S.A.

one

Three things in life made Jill crazy: serious people with so many rules they couldn't relax, panty hose, and a checkbook that wouldn't balance. And here she was, ten dollars short. She'd been staring at the same numbers all morning, scratching her head and chugging coffee so strong it could walk.

She didn't have to worry about serious people because she worked alone. Panty hose were unnecessary in her business. That left only one thing to annoy her. With money as tight as it was, she couldn't afford to be relaxed with her finances. She chewed on the end of her pencil as she perused the numbers again—but with no success.

The bells jingled as the front door opened and closed. Jill glanced up, still in a daze from the numbers that didn't balance, but she forced a smile.

"May I help you with something?" She could barely see him since the sunshine was streaming in the front window behind him. As he came closer, she saw his outdoorsy good looks with short, streaked blond hair, light eyes—were they gray or light blue?—she couldn't quite tell in this lighting—and a natural-looking tan.

He glanced at a slip of paper. "I'm looking for Jill Hargrove." Then he turned to her. "Is she in?" She couldn't help but notice his soft Georgia accent.

Jill lifted one eyebrow. "You're looking at her." This guy sure was cute.

He nodded and extended his hand, which she took only briefly. "I'm Ed Mathis." He stepped back and looked around for a moment before turning to her again. "This is the Junktique Shoppe, right?"

"Right." This guy didn't look anything like what she'd expected. "You're Ed the handyman?"

"Yep. I'm here to fix whatever needs fixin'. Anything that's broken." His eyes crinkled as he smiled.

Jill had expected a much older man, someone with years of experience. Someone who didn't look as if he'd just stepped off the page of a men's catalog. Someone she could work alongside without thinking about how handsome he was.

He gazed around and let out a low chuckle. "Looks like you've got yourself quite a mess here."

Hmm. Jill loved her mess—her collectibles—and she didn't need anyone else calling her place a mess. Suddenly she felt defensive, something that reminded her of worse times, and an awful feeling washed over her. He obviously couldn't tell the difference between vintage collectibles and what he called "a mess." She didn't need negativism. She'd give him a quick and easy job to do and then call the service she'd planned on calling in the first place. The guy in the business next door had meant well when he recommended Ed, but she didn't need someone to judge her and plant seeds of doubt about her lifelong dream.

"Okay," Jill said, looking away. "Let's start with the shelves in the back room. They're about to collapse." That should take a competent handyman a day or two; then she could send him packing.

He nodded. "Let me take a look at 'em."

"C'mon back." She kept her voice calm, but his presence was unnerving.

Jill heard his boots clicking behind her on the hardwood floor. She felt self-conscious in the tattered jeans and ratty T-shirt she'd grabbed on the run this morning. She lifted her hand to the back of her head where her hair had fallen loose from the clip.

"There they are." Jill gestured toward the lopsided shelves she'd installed for extra storage. Ceramic and glass pieces were perched precariously on the shelves, which looked ready to come crashing to the floor at any moment.

Ed whistled and shook his head. "I can tell you now what the problem is. You put too much weight on 'em."

Jill took a step back, placed her hand on her hip, and glared at him. "Excuse me?"

He nodded toward the shelves. "I said, you put too much weight on these shelves."

"I need them for storage. Can you fix them or not?"

He stood still when his gaze met hers, then turned and stared at the wall supporting the shelves before turning back to face her. "I s'pose I could give 'em some support so they can hold all your junk, if you wanna keep piling it on."

"That's not all junk," she said. "Some of it's collectible."

Jill hadn't been sure what to do with these things she'd gotten when bidding on an entire garage filled with Depression glass that was surrounded by. . .junk. Yes, Ed was right, but she couldn't let him know she agreed. Besides, he'd caught her at a very bad time. She was in a lousy mood from the checkbook that wouldn't balance.

"Just do whatever you have to do to fix it," she said. She knew she didn't sound friendly, but this was not a good time.

Ed snorted. "You treat your customers this way?" His look of intense scrutiny caused her to reach up and fidget with her hair again. She knew she must look as if she'd tangled with a bear. "Cuz if you do, they won't keep coming back."

She paused before sniffing and looking him in the eye. "Don't worry about it, Ed. My customers and I get along just fine."

He turned and headed for the door.

"Can you do it?" she called after him.

"Yeah. I just have to go out to my truck for more tools. This job requires more than I can carry on my belt."

"This is not going to work out," Jill mumbled to herself when she was alone. She went to the showroom, straightened a few items, then went behind the checkout counter and moved several things around on the desk. She wondered why Ed was taking so long.

Jill wandered out from behind the desk and glanced out the front window. She saw him pulling an extension ladder from the back of his truck. Then she quickly scurried behind the desk.

The phone rang. "I see Ed made it there." It was Josh Anderson, the neighbor who'd recommended him.

"Yeah, he's here."

"Ed Mathis is the best handyman in the whole Atlanta area," Josh said. "He did quite a bit of renovation in Sandy Springs and Marietta. You'll like his work."

She let out a long sigh. "I'm sure I will. Thanks, Josh."

When Jill got off the phone, Ed returned. "Okay if I prop this door open?" he asked.

"Uh, sure."

Ed fidgeted with the door and figured out a way to make it stay open so he could bring things in from his truck, while Jill straightened some pieces on the shelves. Seconds later, he came walking into the store with the ladder balanced at his side.

"Better be careful with that," she said. "I have some fragile things in here, and I'll—." She stopped short of saying she'd have to charge him. She didn't want to sound mean.

"Don't worry," he said as he went into the back room and extended the ladder, leaning it against the wall. "I'll be careful.

Want to help me get these things out of the way, or are you too busy?"

Without hesitation, Jill was at his side, holding out her hands, reaching for the oversized ceramic rooster he'd lifted from the top shelf. "That piece is very fragile."

Ed snickered. "If you'd left all this stuff up here much longer on the shelves the way they are now, your fragile junk would be in bits and pieces on the floor. I'm surprised it's not already. Now, are you gonna help me find another spot for it so I can fix these shelves, or shall I do it myself?"

"I'll help."

It took them the better part of an hour to get everything down. The anchors she'd tried to brace the shelves with had pulled from the wall, and the toggle bolts were fully exposed and hanging out of the holes in the drywall.

Ed laughed as he pulled the shelves away from the wall. "Whoever put up these shelves didn't know what he was doing."

"For your information, I installed these shelves myself, and I'm not in the mood for your insults."

His shoulders sagged. "Sorry. I didn't mean to come across as insulting."

The bells jingled again. "Customer," she said quickly and hurried away.

Out of the corner of her eye, she could see him watching her for a few seconds as she ran out to see about her customer. Fortunately, now there was a wall section between them, and she wouldn't be tempted to pay more attention to him than to making a sale.

&

Jill's breeze left behind the scent of a blend of sweet flowers and spices. Ed looked at the shelves, which were lopsided on one side and coming apart on the other. He didn't see how someone as petite as Jill had managed to maneuver the shelves enough to bolt them to the wall, even in this slipshod way. He had to hand it to her for trying.

Her defensive nature appeared to be an attempt to hide pain, so he squeezed his eyes shut in a brief prayer that he could do his job without angering her further. Something besides the shop's state of disrepair appeared to be bothering her. He hoped he'd be a good witness throughout this project. Jill was cute, and he loved the way she smelled, but he was pretty sure she had issues.

Ed tried to concentrate on what he needed to do in order to brace the shelves, but he couldn't help but overhear Jill's conversation with the woman in the front of the shop. He moved to get a better view.

Jill's auburn hair was carelessly swept up on top of her head and held with a single clip. Curly strands had fallen loose, and they hung around her face, framing her scrubbed, pale skin and nearly hiding the eyes that had bored a hole through him.

Several times she reached up and took a swipe at her hair, most likely so she could see. He noticed the big brown eyes that were free of makeup, something he suspected she hadn't bothered with because she'd probably just rolled out of bed and thrown herself together to come to work. But that wasn't all he noticed. He was impressed with the respect she showed her customer.

In spite of his resolve to do his work and mind his own business, he was intrigued by this diminutive woman with the obviously kind heart toward the elderly woman she was trying so hard to help. He could tell she had much more patience than he'd ever have with someone who would buy very little, if anything at all, and she seemed to sincerely care about helping that woman.

"I'm not sure we have what you're looking for," she told her customer. "Take a look around and see if anything interests you." She started to walk away, but she stopped when the woman reached out and touched her arm.

The customer asked another question, then chattered incessantly while Jill gave her all her attention. Ed had already grabbed his ladder and was working on steadying it, but he continued to observe. Jill told the woman to let her know if she needed help, and the woman told her she would, thanking her for being such a sweet girl.

Jill glanced over her shoulder and caught Ed staring at her. Ed grabbed his measuring tape and pretended he hadn't been watching her or eavesdropping. Pretending wasn't his strong suit; he'd always been such an up-front guy. He was relieved when the customer came back to the sales desk and put something on the counter. That distracted Jill enough to take the heat off.

"Come back and see me," Jill said as she rang up a purchase Ed couldn't see because he was now hidden on the other side of the wall. He couldn't keep gawking, so he'd actually begun prepping the wall.

"Oh, I will." Then the door opened, letting in the sounds of Atlanta's historic district.

Still distracted, Ed dropped the power drill on his foot and let out a grunt. He bit his bottom lip to absorb some of the pain. Now he was suffering for not paying enough attention to what he was supposed to be doing.

"I bet that hurts," he heard a soft voice say.

Ed glanced up and saw Jill leaning against the doorframe, her arms folded, a slight smile playing on her lips. Now he really felt bad. It had been a mistake to eavesdrop. From now on he'd concentrate on doing the work she'd hired him to do and ignore her—if that was possible.

Josh, one of his buddies from church, had told him Jill

was a single woman who needed a lot of help. *That's an understatement,* Ed thought as he glanced around at the merchandise in the store. What she needed was a bulldozer and a deep landfill.

He shrugged. "Not really."

She took a step closer and looked down at his foot. "You sure?"

"Positive."

The tension in her face faded, and she offered a crooked grin. "Good. Then you'd better pick it up before it starts making a hole in my floor," she said, nodding toward the drill that still lay across his boot.

"It's not even plugged in," Ed said.

"I don't want to take any chances." She turned and walked away, leaving him to deal with his absentmindedness alone. He was pretty sure, but not positive, that she was being playful.

Ed squeezed his eyes shut and prayed silently, *Lord, please give me the strength to know when to open my mouth and when to be silent. I can't do it on my own around this woman.* He opened one eye and saw her profile before closing it again and adding, *She's the cutest boss I've ever had.*

❧

Jill wished she'd gone with her first plan and called someone from the service. The entire time she'd been waiting on her customer she'd been thinking about the man in the back room. When she saw the drill lying on his boot, she resisted the urge to run to him, pick it up, and insist he get off his feet.

One look into his eyes, though, and she backed off. She couldn't afford to let the chemistry between them affect her. She had a career mission, and he would certainly distract her from her goal.

Ed Mathis was only there to fix things in her shop— something any number of handy types could do. She didn't need his critical eye studying her. Okay, she decided, first thing in the morning she'd give him one more thing to do; then she'd pay him, thank him, and send him on his way.

"I have to run out and get some drywall," he said, startling her from her thoughts. "Some of those holes are too big to patch. Besides, I need to add more stud reinforcements behind the drywall, so I might as well start from scratch."

Jill nodded. "Do whatever you have to do. I need those shelves."

He offered her a grin as he raked his fingers through his short-cropped hair. He certainly acted as if he knew what he was doing. Jill had sneaked peeks into the back room to see how he was coming along. He'd cut around the holes where the toggle bolts had pulled out of the wall, then looked inside them with his flashlight, shaking his head and mumbling something she couldn't hear.

After Ed left the shop it was suddenly very quiet. Too quiet. Jill had to flip the switch on her boom box to have something to keep her from thinking too much. She knew every single word of the praise song and sang along. She'd turned it off to balance her checkbook. Music was wonderful when she needed it for creative flow, but when she needed to focus her energy on anything logical, she had to have extreme quiet.

But now wasn't the time to try to balance her checkbook. Logic had taken a hike after Ed walked in. Jill knew she needed to learn plenty of things, but she wanted to do it without someone hovering over her, watching. He had already shown signs of being too much like her father—organized and meticulous to a fault. He'd measured every single angle on the wall where the shelves had fallen. Even his toolbox was organized and labeled.

A couple of regular customers came and went, each of them buying a few pieces for their collections, but not enough to make a significant improvement in her bank balance. In the short time Jill had been in business, she'd developed relationships with people who came into the shop. They'd found her shop mostly from the small ads she'd placed in the local collectors' newsletter. To stay in business, she knew it would take a lot more than the handful of collectors who'd found the Junktique Shoppe.

Jill glanced at her watch every couple of minutes, wondering what was taking Ed so long. When he finally came back, she let out a deep sigh. Okay, so she liked having him there. That was the main reason he needed to go.

"How's your foot?"

Ed shook his head. "Foot's fine."

"Good."

She glanced out the window at his loaded truck. "How much will this cost?" Jill asked.

He smiled. "I'll give you a little discount."

Now she was even more worried. "I didn't ask for a discount."

"This needs to be done right, and from the look of things you can't afford the full price." He set his jaw, widened his stance, and folded his arms. "I don't know if Josh told you, but I don't do things halfway."

Yes, Josh had told her, which was why she had chosen Ed.

"Okay," she finally said while doing a quick mental calculation of how many days in a row she could eat boxed mac and cheese. "Do whatever you have to do to get those shelves up. But that might be all I can afford." There was no point in hiding the fact that she was a struggling new business owner. He'd figure it out soon enough anyway.

The bells on the front door sounded again, so Jill left Ed and concentrated on taking care of her customers. The young couple told her they had just bought an old house in the heart of Atlanta and were looking for pieces for their new place.

"I don't want department-store, cookie-cutter kinds of things," the woman said. "I want my first house to have character."

The man behind her nodded, clearly smitten with his wife. If Jill had to guess, she'd say they were a newly married couple, perhaps right out of college.

"Take a look around," Jill told them. "If you see something you like, I'll be glad to help you. Or if you have something in mind that you don't see, I'll write it down and call you if anything like it comes in."

The woman beamed. "Thanks so much." Turning to the man, she said, "C'mon, honey. I can already tell this is my favorite antique store."

By the time they'd gone from one side of the front sales floor to the other, the woman had piled the man's arms with so many trinkets and knickknacks, he couldn't have held more if he'd wanted to. Jill came to their rescue.

"Here—let me take those things so you can shop some more. Have you been upstairs?"

The woman's face lit up. "There's more?"

Jill nodded. "I have a whole floor of nothing but ceramic and porcelain."

As soon as the couple went upstairs, Ed came out from behind the back wall. "I was wrong about this place."

Jill jumped. He'd startled her. "What?"

"I just said I was wrong. When I first walked in here, I thought this place was doomed to failure. I'd never seen so much junk under one roof in my life."

She felt an overwhelming sense of pride, not to mention the fact that she enjoyed his praise.

Before she had a chance to comment, he continued. "Apparently you've found a niche market, and because of that you'll be quite successful." The respect in his voice took some of the bite out of his first comment.

"You really think so?"

He nodded. "If you can keep your head above water for the first couple of years, I have no doubt this place will be a raging success."

Tilting her head to one side, she squinted as she studied him. "How would you know this sort of thing?"

"Business experience," he replied as he turned his back on her. "Lots of it."

❧

Ed thought she knew who he was, but apparently not. He could tell she thought he was just a neighborhood handyman.

His business, Mathis Construction, just happened to be the most successful home improvement company in north Georgia. His specialty was restoring old homes. Only recently he had decided to develop a brand-new neighborhood up in the Ackworth area, but the zoning would take months, which freed him up to do odd jobs here and there. He also welcomed a break from the long ten- and twelve-hour days spent working on a project of that magnitude. Handy work was something he actually enjoyed for a change of pace. Ed had figured he'd take a break and spend more time with his twin daughters, who were becoming a huge handful. He'd accepted this short-term job as a favor to his friend Josh, who said a very sweet, young entrepreneur needed a little help getting started. Now he found himself wondering about her spiritual side. She seemed defensive and troubled.

He wanted to run before getting involved with her, but his conscience and faith wouldn't let him. She might be good with customers, but this place was ready to be condemned.

The whole place was falling apart. The first thing he'd noticed was how the wooden planks of the porch floor were rotten—a lawsuit waiting to happen. The inside wasn't any better. He'd seen evidence of termites, but he wasn't yet sure if any live ones were in the building.

Another thing Ed needed to talk to her about was holding on to her profits. He'd overheard her offering huge discounts to people who seemed willing to buy at full price.

With the drywall and two-by-fours lined up, Ed began ripping away the existing drywall, exposing everything behind it. That was when he saw how the wiring was brittle and cracking in some places. And there they were. Live termites. If they were localized to one area, they could be spot treated. But if they were as bad as he'd seen in other houses, she'd need to have this place tented.

He took a step back and inspected what was in front of him. It was much worse than he'd thought. Most likely the whole place needed rewiring, a project he'd have to subcontract out to a licensed electrician. From the looks of things, this house hadn't been the best investment for a young businesswoman who didn't know a thing about repairs. He wondered why the bank had allowed the loan to go through with all the problems he spotted.

Ed narrowed his eyes as he considered his options. Should he repair the wall and ignore the wiring? No, he couldn't do that. Should he tell Jill what he'd noticed and duck? Her stress level was already high enough. Then there was the other option, one he'd tried to push from his mind. Plenty of people from church would help out if he asked them to, but somehow he doubted the prickly Jill would accept that offer.

"Something wrong?" she asked as she came around and caught him deep in thought.

Ed's heart twisted as he noticed the expectant look on her face. She was waiting for an answer.

two

Her initial reaction was exactly what he'd expected. She admitted she'd put all her money into the place, and it was paid for free and clear, so she hadn't gone through the traditional bank financing. The owner had obviously sold it to her "as is" and rushed her through the process, which should have alerted her to something being wrong. But it was too late to go into that now.

Her face turned a deep shade of red. Then she offered a sheepish smile.

"I should have had this place inspected before I closed on it," she said softly. "I bet you think I'm stupid."

"No, I don't think you're stupid." He paused and held her gaze until she quickly looked away. "Just very eager to go into business for yourself."

She swallowed hard. "Thank you for understanding."

Sensing she needed her space, Ed stepped outside and called his best friend from church, an electrician he'd met on a job years ago. He explained the situation. "Any way you can come right over?" he asked.

"I'm just now leaving today's job. I'll be there in a half hour," Matt said.

"Be careful," Ed warned. "She's fragile."

"She? You mean the shop?"

"Yeah, that too, but I was talking about the owner."

Matt chuckled. "I can handle fragile women. Trust me."

Ed hung up and said a prayer of thanks for his friend. Then he prayed for more guidance with Jill.

When Matt arrived, Ed left him to inspect the wiring while he moved on to the next area that needed repairing.

"You sure you wanna cover this?" Matt asked after a few minutes. "It'll cost you some bucks."

Ed looked at the frayed wires Matt held in both hands. Slowly he nodded.

Matt grinned. "She must be pretty special, Ed. I had no idea you were getting serious about some girl. How long has this been going on?"

"Nothing's going on, Matt. I just met her this morning."

"Whoa!" Matt said as he took a step back. "Run that one by me again."

"You heard me."

"Why are you about to plunk down some hefty change to rewire this house, then? She hired you to do work for her, which means she's supposed to pay you. Not the other way around."

A long silence fell between the men. "Yes, I know," Ed finally replied. "Just wait until you get to know her. You'll see."

Matt chuckled. "Okay, then. First I have to pull out all the existing wires, then snake new ones through to the same locations. And most likely the breaker box will need replacing, too."

Ed knew Matt would come to the rescue.

"There isn't a breaker box. This house is old, Matt. It still has fuses."

"Fuse box has never been replaced?"

"Nope."

"Then we'll definitely have to put in a breaker box." He rocked back on his heels, then rubbed his neck. "Seeing as how you're doing this for charity, I'll donate my time and just charge you for materials."

"Donate your time for what?" a female voice said from the doorway.

Ed glanced up to see Jill staring at him, a curious look on her face. He'd thought she was upstairs, helping some customers. Obviously not.

Matt shot Ed a panic-stricken glance, then turned away, leaving Ed to do damage control. "Uh. . ."

Narrowing her gaze, Jill shook her head. "I'm not asking for charity. I pay my way. Nothing's free."

Ed held out his hands. "C'mon, Jill. It's not that big a deal. We're just tryin' to help. We do that a lot for each other."

"Yeah, but you've got a friendship for who knows how long. I just met both of you."

"How long do we have to know each other before we can say we're friends?" Ed challenged. "Just because you and I only met today doesn't make us any less friends, does it?"

Jill didn't say anything as he tried to find the right words. Finally she sighed. "Maybe we can work something out."

"Work something out?" Ed asked.

"Yeah," she replied. "Like a two-way deal. If you and this guy"—she said, nodding toward Matt, who was pretending not to listen—"want to do some work for me, then I want to do something for you in return."

"Like what?"

"I can cook."

Matt suddenly spun around. "And I like to eat. It's a deal."

With a shrug Ed said, "Okay, sounds like a pretty good plan. We do the work around here and only charge for materials. You can cook a meal for us."

"Not just a meal," she said slowly. "Dinner for a month."

Ed thought about his daughters and his responsibility of feeding them each night. Oh, well, he'd work out something. For now he'd be agreeable.

"Fine," he said with a grunt.

"Sounds good," Matt said as he backed away, moving toward

the door. "I'll see ya first thing in the mornin', Ed."

After he was gone, Jill closed her eyes and blew out a deep breath. "You okay?" Ed asked.

She nodded. "How bad is it?"

"The wiring in this house is shot, Jill, just like quite a few other things. I don't think the plumbing's in good shape, either."

She leaned against the wall and closed her eyes.

"Everything will work out," he said as he took a step closer. Her face had gone pasty white.

"I don't have any idea how I'm going to pull any of this off. My father died eight months ago and left me barely enough money to buy a small home and this old house, which I thought was the perfect location for the business I've always wanted."

Ed felt a heaviness in his chest. Now he felt more compelled than ever to do something to help her out. No wonder she was frustrated. This was her inheritance.

"I'm really sorry," he said.

"Why are you sorry?" She sniffled. "The fact that this house is falling apart isn't your fault."

Ed rubbed the back of his neck. "I'm sorry to hear about your father." He held up his hands and gestured around the room. "I'm sorry this place is such a wreck."

She shrugged as she pulled a tissue from her pocket and blew her nose. "Maybe I should just have it condemned and move on."

The sound of desperation in her voice kicked him in the gut. "Whatever you want to do, just let me know before we go any further." He took a small step back, then stopped. "I didn't mean that. This place has to be fixed. I'm not leaving until it's done." No way would he leave her in the lurch.

Jill glanced up at him with a questioning look. "What?"

"I said I'm not leaving. In fact I'm sticking around until every last thing in this place is taken care of."

What had he just committed to? Days, maybe even weeks or months, of hard work and time that would most likely go unpaid? He had plenty of money to last him until he started on the new housing and commercial development—that wasn't the point. But this was supposed to be a little hiatus for him between major remodeling jobs and the new development.

Jill had opened her mouth, but she shut it again as she hung her head. Ed knew she was scared. And she should be. All her money was tied up in a place she'd never be able to sell if someone had the sense to hire an inspector before buying it—as *she* should have done.

"We need to start with the foundation and wiring first," Ed offered when he saw that she was speechless.

"Look, Ed," Jill finally said. "I know all the dinners I can cook for you and your friends won't be enough to pay for the work this place needs." Glancing around frantically, she said, "I'll pay you a little bit each month until it's paid off."

He didn't want to take money from her, but he wasn't about to take away every last shred of her pride, either. Nodding slowly, he replied, "Okay, it's a deal, but only for the materials. We'll exchange labor for dinners."

"Keep track of everything," she said as she looked directly at him with big brown eyes that sent his heart into overdrive.

"You bet I will."

And he meant it, too. He would keep track of absolutely everything—from her soulful eyes, her creamy skin, her hair that was in desperate need of brushing, all the way to her pink-painted toenails that peeked out from her sturdy sandals.

Keeping track of the cost of the project was altogether another thing, though. He was certain that some of the material receipts might get "lost" somewhere along the way.

Jill scooted away from Ed and made her way across the room. Ed was staring down at his boots when he noticed she'd stopped by the door to the front sales floor.

He looked up and found her staring back at him. "Is there something else?" he asked.

"Yeah," she replied. "I was wondering why you're doing this."

He was stumped. How can a man describe that overwhelming urge to protect a creature he barely knew? The Lord had brought him here to help her, but he wasn't sure if she was ready to hear that. So he tried to act nonchalant. "I'm just a nice guy, I guess."

"Uh-huh," she said as she disappeared around the corner.

Ed felt awful for not jumping on the opportunity to witness. Hurrying after her, he said, "There's something you need to know, Jill."

"What?" She stopped and issued a challenging stare.

"Matt and I are in the same Bible study group from church. We have a few more friends from church who are in the building business, and I want to get them to help out, too."

She closed her eyes for a few seconds, then looked directly into his. "So you're doing this because of your faith?"

"Well, sort of. As Christians, we're supposed to help others—even people who don't believe the same way we do."

"So you think I'm not a believer?"

"Are you?"

"Yes."

Her one-word statement gave him a rush of pleasure.

"Then you understand why we want to help you," he said.

"I've already said I'm not a charity case."

Ed wanted to remind her that everyone was a charity case, and Jesus had to bail them out of their own depravity. But she didn't appear to be in a listening mood at the moment. He chose to take a more tactful approach and save the best for another time.

"We're getting meals, remember?"

"Trust me, I won't forget."

"Do you have a church home?"

She shook her head. "No, but I read my Bible daily."

"Would you like to be my guest at Good Shepherd?"

She paused for a couple of seconds. "Maybe later," she finally said before walking away to tend to a customer.

Ed managed to get the area cleaned up enough so he wouldn't face a mess in the morning. The gaping hole in the wall was still there, but he needed to leave it alone in order for Matt to have full access to what he hoped would be the worst part of the electrical problem.

Most of the old drywall had been hauled outside and the new drywall stacked when Jill came back, took a long assessing look around the room, and shook her head.

"You'll be fine," Ed said. "Matt's good at what he does, and he'll fix you right up." He glanced her way and saw those big, trusting, brown eyes looking at him. Now his heart was involved. How could a man turn away from that?

❧

Jill hated feeling vulnerable and helpless. Her father had been a powerful man in the military, and then he'd come home and expected her to accept the orders he barked at her. She had known that because she depended on him, she had to do things his way. But she'd promised herself that once she was grown and out on her own, she'd never put herself in a defenseless position again.

Yet here she was, depending on a man to take care of her. Ed was sweet; she still didn't like the fact that she'd owe him something, though, even if it was only meals and the money he'd have to front for the materials.

She stood and watched him clean up, not saying a word. His silence left her wondering what he was thinking, but she was glad he chose not to make idle chitchat.

Finally he stood and brushed his hands off on the front of his jeans. "What time do you get here in the morning?" he asked.

She shrugged. "The store opens at ten. Sometime around then."

He tilted his head and looked puzzled.

"Why are you looking at me like that?" she asked as the heat rose to her neck.

"Don't you come early to set up or get ready for business?" he asked.

"It's not necessary."

Jill had to step back to keep from being too heavily scrutinized by those gray-blue eyes that seemed to penetrate her thoughts. She stumbled over a quilted stuffed animal she'd dropped yesterday but had forgotten to pick up and put away. That only made it worse. She wanted simply to tell him it was none of his business when she arrived at the store, but that wasn't the case. She knew he probably wanted to get an early start.

He glanced down at the stuffed animal then back at her. She tried to look away, but his gaze held hers.

"I reckon that'll be okay," he said, surprising her. "I have a few things to do down at city hall anyway."

"Okay, so I'll be here early tomorrow, but don't expect me to make a habit of it," Jill said as she turned toward the front of the store.

"I never asked you to—," he began.

"No, you didn't," she conceded, interrupting him. "But if that'll get this whole project over with faster, I'll work with you this once. What time do you want to get started?"

"Seven."

"*Seven?*" she shrieked. "I won't even be up at seven."

With a shrug Ed said, "Okay, what time do you want me to be here?"

Jill glanced down at her feet, thought for a moment, then looked at the wall behind him, not daring to meet his gaze again. It was too dangerous.

"I'll be here at seven."

He chuckled. "I've already told you this job will take a few weeks. If you trust me enough to give me a key, I can let myself in."

Jill gulped then nodded. "I'll have it for you in the morning."

The moment Ed left, the place seemed empty. Most of the remainder of the afternoon was slow, with the exception of a few stragglers, one of them Mrs. Crenshaw, who came in once a week and purchased every piece of milk glass Jill had been able to find. As soon as she'd wrapped the order and carried it to Mrs. Crenshaw's car, Jill glanced at one of her many clocks and decided she could go ahead and leave now. The sign on the door said she was open until six, and she still had fifteen minutes to go, but she was mentally exhausted.

She grabbed her purse and backed toward the door. Maybe tomorrow she could work on the checkbook and figure out where the ten-dollar mistake was since she'd be here before the store opened. She'd planned to call the bank today, but Ed Mathis had distracted her, and it was too late now; the bank was closed.

Oh, well. Jill started to pull the door to, then remembered her keys were on the counter. She shoved the door open, ran across the wooden plank floor, grabbed the keys, and headed for the door again. When she got to the porch, she saw a familiar male figure coming up the sidewalk.

"Closing for the day?" Ed asked as he took a glance at his watch. "A little early, isn't it?"

"It's my business, and I can leave whenever I feel like it."

"So why do you even bother posting hours on the sign?" he asked, nodding toward the wooden plaque on the door. "Instead of saying you're open from ten to six, you should have said you open whenever you get here and leave whenever you feel like it."

Jill reached up and shoved an annoying strand of hair behind her ear. "Hey, don't worry about it, Ed."

"I'm not worried," he said. "But wouldn't it be a shame to miss out on a big sale just because you didn't stick around until closing time?"

"Why?" she asked as she stopped in her tracks. "You planning on buying something big?"

He shrugged and hooked his thumbs in his belt loops. "Maybe."

She fumbled with her keys. "Want me to open back up?"

"Nah," he said as he continued looking at her in a way that made her very uncomfortable. Those eyes seemed to be all-knowing, his mouth set in a perpetual tilt of amusement, not to mention the fact that he was very handsome in an almost too-perfect sort of way. His hair was clean and freshly cut and his jeans appeared to have been ironed, maybe even starched.

Jill glanced down at her own tattered jeans. They weren't dirty, but they'd never seen an iron. And her T-shirt had been a promotional giveaway from the bank when she'd opened her account. His shirt had a collar and an emblem on the pocket. They were obviously polar opposites.

As if to drive the point home, another strand of hair fell over her eyes. Ed reached over and gently tucked it behind her ear. What was up with that? She stepped back and shook her head, letting the strand fall loose again. She tilted her head to one side and watched him grimace. Served him right for being too persnickety. Without a word, she headed toward her car.

"Don't forget to have a key made," he said as he watched her unlock her car that was parked along the side of the curb. "That is, if you trust me."

"I'll have it made sometime tomorrow," she said. "Probably during lunch."

"Sounds good." Ed remained standing on the sidewalk.

She wished he'd leave or at least turn around.

"I need to run. The nanny can't stay past six."

"Nanny?" She stopped cold in her tracks.

He nodded. "Yeah, I have twin daughters."

"You do?" She didn't know he was attached, but what should that matter? "You're married?"

He shook his head. "My wife developed complications during her pregnancy and died after she delivered them. As soon as I was able to get back to work, I had to hire a nanny."

She swallowed hard. "I'm sorry. It's none of my business. I'm really sorry. Sometimes I say stupid—"

"That's okay." Ed's smile was tender. "My girls and I are just fine."

Jill didn't know what to do, so she smiled back. Now she felt even more awkward.

It had been a very long time since Jill had been self-conscious because, quite frankly, she hardly ever cared what a man thought about her. She was what she was, and she wasn't about to change her ways.

Her perfectionist father had been such a stickler. He'd ruined any desire she might've had for ever wanting to dress up or do housework, which was why her shop and her house both looked as if someone had shaken them and left things where they'd landed. But that was the way she liked her life, and it was too bad if someone thought she was a mess.

Her small house was situated on a narrow, tree-lined residential road off Peachtree Street, about a mile from the shop. She'd decided to start out small, and as the shop grew she would reassess her life and maybe get something nicer or fix up her place. For now, though, the cottage with the overgrown yard was perfect for her. One of these days she planned to do something about the shaggy shrubs and the weeds in the flower garden. She'd already pulled up some of the kudzu, because one of the neighbors had warned her how it would take over everything else if she didn't. But that's where she stopped. She had other things to fill her time for now.

Since her driveway was covered in weeds and she didn't want to take a chance on getting a flat tire from whatever else lay in the path, she didn't bother parking in the carport in the backyard by the alley. She pulled up and parallel-parked at the curb in front of her house.

The front porch still needed a coat of paint, something she'd intended to do first thing when she moved in, but she hadn't gotten around to yet. Even if it never got done, as far as Jill was concerned, it was no big deal.

She had no doubt all of this would annoy Ed. He was obviously a perfectionist—just like her father, which was the biggest reason she needed to keep her emotions in check.

Jill slipped the key in the lock and turned it as she jiggled the handle to open the door. This thing always stuck. Almost everything in Jill's life stuck, creaked, or squeaked. She was used to it.

Once inside her tiny house, Jill flipped on the switch. The ceiling light cast a dull glow over the room. She hadn't bothered picking up her blanket from the sofa, where she'd fallen asleep the night before. *Oh, well, let it stay there,* she thought. She'd need it again tonight.

Ever since Jill had started her business, she'd had a hard time falling asleep in her bed. So she reclined on the sofa and watched late-night talk shows, which had become so boring and predictable she was eventually able to go to sleep. This pattern would be a tough one to break, but that didn't matter. Jill lived alone, and she could do anything she pleased.

Her father would turn over in his grave if he could see how his daughter lived amidst all this clutter. His motto had been, "Everything has its place."

Sure, at times Jill felt guilty that she'd abandoned her upbringing and his rules, but he was gone and couldn't see it anyway. So what did it matter?

Dishes were still piled in the sink from breakfast, so she opened the dishwasher and shoved them all inside to expose a little counter space. Maybe she'd run a load soon and put them away. Or maybe she'd just leave them in the dishwasher and pull them out as needed. What did it matter?

She popped a frozen dinner in the microwave and left the kitchen to find her collectibles magazine to read while she ate. By the time she returned to the kitchen the buzzer had gone off, letting her know her food was ready.

Although this wasn't the way she'd envisioned her life, Jill was perfectly content. . .well, most of the time, anyway. No unnecessary rules; no one to tell her where to be or when to be there; no restrictions on food or someone standing over her making sure she had three squares. Just her life to be lived the way she wanted.

She wasn't lonely.

Jill sighed. Who was she trying to kid? She'd give her favorite knickknack to have someone to talk to right now. Someone who understood her and cared enough to listen.

"Oh, well, it's not going to happen anytime soon," she mumbled to herself. She picked the magazine back up and forced herself to look at it.

As she flipped the pages, she noticed how neatly the items in the pictures were arranged. Once Ed finished building her shelves in the back room, she could do a much better job of organizing her merchandise and have arrangements ready to be placed on the shelves.

Suddenly she slammed the magazine shut. Once his image had popped into her head, she wasn't able to get rid of it. She so needed a break—which included not thinking about the man who reminded her way too much of her father and his neatnik ways.

Jill let out a sigh. It was still early enough that she could probably head for the mall and find someone to duplicate the key to the store. Any work Ed did before she arrived would put him that much closer to completing the job and getting him out of there. He had daughters. That one fact alone was a good enough reason to stop thinking about him. She did not need to worry, or even think, about children—too much responsibility.

&

Ed fully expected to have to wait for Jill, but he reached the store bright and early the next morning. He'd picked up a sack of muffins on the way so he could have breakfast under the big oak tree outside the shop and enjoy the early morning hours.

Life was so busy these days that he loved taking a few minutes here and there to enjoy some of God's blessings. There was nothing better than the sounds and smells of early morning. *Animals work hard for survival,* he thought, as a squirrel scampered by, carrying a nut to the next tree. He inhaled deeply and relished the freshness of the crisp north Georgia air. Fall had arrived, but a few protected floral stragglers remained in the yard around Jill's shop. Ed loved everything about the Atlanta area—from the terrain to the variety of people who'd made it their home.

"You weren't kidding, were you?" he heard from behind.

He licked his lips and swallowed the last bite of his muffin.

"I never expected to see you here this early."

She rolled her eyes and shook her head. "Then why did you come? For the thrill of making me feel guilty for making you wait?"

"Maybe," he teased.

Jill brushed past him and headed straight for the door. She shoved her key in hard and turned it. She had to lean into the door to get it to open; then it creaked.

"That probably just needs some WD-40," he said.

"Whatever." Jill reached over and flipped a light switch, then went to the counter and dropped her purse and the other bag she was carrying on the floor. She spun around and held up something shiny. "Here's your key."

Ed smiled as he reached for the key he thought he'd never have. "So you do trust me after all."

three

Ed felt an overwhelming urge to reach out and take her hand, to assure her he was trustworthy.

He would never do anything to hurt any client, especially her. In the short time he'd known her, his protective nature had kicked into high gear.

"Is there any reason why I shouldn't trust you?" she asked, her voice low and unsure.

"No reason at all, Jill. C'mon—let me show you what we have to do." His voice cracked.

Jill's eyes grew rounder as she followed him from room to room.

"This is going to cost me a fortune, even if I'm only charged for materials," she said with a groan. "And I'm sunk."

"Not necessarily," he said. "It's not as bad as it seems. The only thing you have to remember is to let me do my job. As a builder I get construction materials at wholesale."

She finally sighed and nodded. "Okay, do what you have to do. I have to trust you."

Ed felt his chest constrict. He wanted her trust more than he'd realized.

Less than an hour later Matt showed up. "Finish it quickly," Ed quietly told him. "Keep in mind Jill's getting a little nervous about all this. Whatever you do, don't let on how much it costs. Just give me the bill, okay?"

Matt grinned. "She's your new pet project, huh?" Ed's friends had always teased him about wanting to rescue people in distress. Matt leaned back, looked at the woman with the wild curls piled on top of her head, then glanced back at Ed. "Not bad, Ed. She's really cute. You could do much worse."

Ed knew Matt couldn't possibly understand the conflicting feelings he had for Jill. Even *he* didn't fully understand them. Yes, he was attracted to her; but, no, he wasn't about to act on his feelings.

But he wasn't able to get her out of his mind, either, even when a wall stood between them. Her innocent and trusting expressions chipped away at the shield he'd placed over his heart after his wife died. He tightened his jaw. Being around Jill evoked a feeling he hadn't experienced in a very long time.

Each time he caught a whiff of her spicy fragrance, he found his mind drifting into territory he'd been avoiding since Marcy died. After all he'd gone through with losing his wife, Ed felt it was best to guard against any chance of losing his heart again.

"Ed!" he heard Jill holler from the front room. "I hate to bother you, but could you come in here a minute?"

He propped the sheet of drywall he'd been working with against a stud and rushed to see what she needed. When he got to the door, he saw her standing dangerously close to the edge of the top rung of a stepladder, reaching as high as her arms would go, but still not high enough to get the ceramic rooster off the top shelf.

"Don't you know you're not supposed to stand on the top step?" He offered her a hand.

"I really need that rooster," she said as she took his hand and cautiously stepped down.

"Okay." Ed helped her down, then moved the ladder to one side.

"Hey, what are you doing?" she asked. "Even you can't reach that without a ladder."

Ed moved quickly to the back room, grabbed the taller ladder, and hoisted it into place. "If you're gonna stick stuff up that high, I suggest you get the equipment you need."

"You're the one who put it back up there."

"Only because you wanted it there," he replied as gently as he could.

She placed her hands on her hips and watched him. Her eyes showed a combination of emotions besides frustration—anger, relief, and maybe even a little admiration—as he grabbed hold of the rooster and began to descend the ladder.

"Hey, be careful with that. That thing cost me a fortune."

Ed chuckled. "Who woulda guessed?"

As soon as Ed offered it to her, Jill reached for it. "Don't pass judgment on something you know nothing about," she said as their fingers touched.

The tight sensation in his chest should have served as a warning to keep his distance, but the look in her eyes held him captive for a few seconds—just long enough for him to lose his breath.

Jill glanced down at the floor as she took a step back, nearly falling over the basket that lay on the floor behind her. Ed caught her just in time.

"Whoa there," he said as he cupped his palms beneath her elbows.

He refrained from saying anything about the clutter on the floor. That wouldn't serve any purpose at the moment, and he knew it.

To keep her from falling, he instinctively pulled her to him. She was still hanging on to the rooster, which slammed him in the chest.

"Ouch!" he said. He let go and inhaled deeply. "That thing's lethal."

Jill tilted her head and glared at him. "You're determined to make me feel stupid, aren't you?"

"Why would you say that?"

She backed toward the counter and carefully set the rooster down. "First of all, you tell me I can't build sturdy enough shelves to hold my excess stock. Then you tell me this place is falling apart and that my investment is worthless. And now you're making fun of what I sell. I'll have you know—"

Ed held up his hands to shush her. "Stop right there, Jill. I'm just here to do a job. I didn't mean to insult you."

"But you did."

"I'm sorry."

She sniffed. That protective feeling still hadn't left Ed. He shuffled his feet and tried to redirect his thoughts.

"Apology accepted."

"You asked me to help you get something down off the top shelf. If you want me to stay away from you, just tell me right now."

She blinked a couple of times, but to his surprise she didn't say anything.

❧

Jill couldn't remember the last time she'd shown her emotions in front of a man. Her father had forbidden her to shed tears, because he said it was a sign of weakness. After practicing keeping a stiff upper lip, Jill couldn't imagine letting her fears be known to someone she'd only met yesterday.

This business was what she'd dreamed of all her life. Her grandmother had had a house filled with knickknacks and fun little figurines that delighted Jill from her earliest memory. Moving around from one military base to another had prevented her from collecting all the items she'd loved as a child. So she'd promised to surround herself with pretty and fun things when she was grown. Her own collections had inspired her desire to be in the collectibles business, where she could talk to and help people with common interests all day long.

Opening the Junktique Shoppe had been like a dream come true, until she realized she wasn't capable of doing everything that needed to be done around here. Her underestimation of the cost of a business could ruin her before she had a chance. She'd had no idea how much utilities were before she'd actually had them turned on. All she'd figured on was the price of the building and purchasing items for resale. Going into business for herself was like being doused with a bucket of ice water when reality kicked in.

Being self-employed beat working for someone else. But it wasn't nearly as much fun as she'd thought it would be because of the hard, cold, money issues.

Now her handyman—her kindhearted, great-looking handyman with the penetrating eyes that could see through her facade—was trying to save her from herself.

She'd put everything into this business. A nice, elderly woman from the Greater Atlanta Small Business Administration had given her some advice and helped her to work up a plan. She would do her best to stick to it, despite the bad news about the building.

"The biggest reason businesses fail is that the owners don't make plans and stick to them," the woman had said. "You'll have to tighten your belt, but if you can get through the first couple of years, you'll do just fine."

But what if she wasn't able to make it through the first couple of years? Everything her father had left her would go down the drain if the Junktique Shoppe failed. And if she kept throwing her profit into fixing this dilapidated house, she was certain to face bankruptcy in no time.

Maybe she should have stayed in her apartment in Dallas, kept her receptionist job with the small advertising agency, and invested her inheritance money for retirement. That would have been the safe thing to do. Much safer to her heart, at least, than facing this man every day for the next few weeks. But she would always have felt a pull to the place her mother loved and wanted to return to until the day she'd passed away.

Her mother used to tell her about Atlanta and how wonderful it was. She had talked about the people from all over who came together in the sprawling metropolis, the beautiful terrain, the shopping, and the Varsity, which at that time laid claim to being the biggest fast-food restaurant in the world. When she got to Atlanta, the first thing Jill did was go to the Varsity and order a frosted orange and some onion rings.

Fearful of having Ed look at her again, Jill turned away from him as she said, "Thanks, Ed."

"No problem."

The sound of his boots on the hardwood floor let her know he was walking away from her. Now she could relax and get on with the business of figuring out the error in her checkbook.

Jill chewed on the tip of her mechanical pencil, studying the rows of numbers in the bank book, still confused over where ten dollars could have gone. She was so deep in thought, she jumped when she heard the sound from the other side of the counter.

"Didn't mean to scare you," he said. "Having a problem?"

"Uh, yeah," she admitted. After all, it had to be obvious she wasn't having fun.

"Mechanical pencils aren't made for gnawing," he said with a half smile, one corner of his lips lifted in a make-my-day tilt.

She blew out a breath. "I just hate when my books don't balance."

A snort escaped Ed's lips. "I never would have figured you for the balanced-checkbook sort of gal."

"What?" She looked at him with a squint.

Right when she was ready to defend herself, Ed glanced down, then looked back up at her. "Sorry," he said. "That was totally uncalled-for. Sometimes I stick my foot in my mouth and say stupid things."

All the fighting wind had been blown from Jill's sail. "Hey, don't worry about it. I understand." And she did. Everything else in her life was in chaos. Why wouldn't he think her checkbook would be, too?

Nodding toward the checkbook, Ed said, "Mind if I take a look at that? I'm pretty good with numbers."

She hesitated for a moment then pushed it toward him. What harm was there in letting him see what she had—or didn't have—in her business account? He wasn't blind. He could see she was struggling.

Ed hadn't been looking at her checkbook more than a couple of minutes when his friends started to arrive. One by one Jill met them, and she found herself amazed by their kindness and eagerness to get started right away.

☙

At the end of a long, whirlwind day, Ed showed Jill where her checking account error was. The bank had coded one of her checks improperly. It was their error, not hers. Fortunately, catching the mistake was in her favor. "Thanks so much, Ed," she told him more than once as he gathered his tools and began stacking things while getting ready to leave for the day.

"No problem," he replied. "I need to get home soon. My daughters' nanny has to leave early today, and I can't be late."

He noticed how she visibly tensed at the mention of his daughters. She didn't appear wild about children, which was another very good reason to keep his emotional distance from her. Although he was attracted to Jill, he knew he couldn't get involved with her. He and his girls were part of a package, making it even more difficult to think about getting into a relationship. Not many women were prepared for two very lively preschoolers who could outsmart most adults.

After Ed left the shop he headed straight home. The girls had their noses pressed against the big picture window in the living room. Suddenly their little faces disappeared from the window; then the two reappeared at the front door.

"Daddy!" Stacy said as she flung open the door. She threw herself into his arms, while her twin sister, the more demure Tracy, pulled at his hand. "We're starving."

Mrs. Cooper, the nanny, already had her purse hooked over her arm. "Sorry to do this to you, Mr. Mathis, but I really must go. I thawed the ground beef as you asked me to."

"Thanks," he told her. "See you in the morning."

The second she was gone, Stacy piped up. "Daddy, we wanna go to the Varsity for chili cheese dogs."

"I thought we'd cook hamburgers on the grill tonight."

"Let's do that tomorrow," Stacy said. "I want a chili cheese dog."

"That okay with you, Tracy?" he asked as he glanced down at his other daughter. She nodded. "Okay, Varsity it is. We'll cook out tomorrow night."

"Can I have french fries?"

Ed blew out a sigh. "You can have whatever you want, Stacy."

"What'd you do today, Daddy?" Tracy asked after he fastened them both into their car seats in the backseat of the cab of his truck.

"Well," he began, "there's this really interesting shop I've been helping restore." Then he told them about the Junktique Shoppe while they listened, paying close attention to every word he said.

Finally Stacy said, "Is she pretty?"

Ed squinted. "Is who pretty?"

"The lady. Jill."

"Oh, her. Yeah, I guess she's pretty."

With a quick glance in the rearview mirror, he could see

Tracy turn around and look at her sister, a smile quirking her face. "I wanna see her," Stacy said.

He should have figured as much. "Maybe later."

"When?"

"How about when I finish the job?"

Ed knew from experience he needed to change the subject quickly, or he'd have to answer more questions about Jill. They took the bait, but he knew this wasn't the last he'd hear from his daughters.

After they got home from the Varsity he helped them with their baths, read stories to them, tucked them into their beds, and said prayers with them. "Love you, girls," he said, backing toward the door.

"Love you, too, Daddy," they said in unison.

Later on that night Ed lay in his own bed, thinking about the progress he'd made at the shop. He had an odd sensation about Jill. Something besides the state of disrepair of her shop was going on with her. What had happened to cause her so much worry?

Maybe the Lord had brought Ed into Jill's life for a reason other than fixing her shop. He wasn't sure about much in his life, but he did know one thing: Whenever things didn't make sense to him, he needed to be quiet and let the Lord take over. He prayed for guidance. Being there for Jill didn't mean he needed to get romantically involved with her; he'd have to be very careful not to let that happen.

When he arrived at the shop the next morning, two of his friends were there, waiting for someone to unlock the door. "We thought you'd never get here," Matt said.

"I had to wait for the nanny." Ed unlocked the door to let them in. "Before we get started I want to tell you guys something."

They huddled in the corner while he explained his mission

and how he suspected Jill needed more than handy work in her shop. They nodded their understanding and promised they'd watch for opportunities to pray for her.

"Just remember," he said, "we have to be very gentle. I suspect there's something deep going on."

By the time Jill arrived, the three men were well into their tasks. She grinned as Ed greeted her.

"Wow!" she said. "You told me you'd be fast, but I had no idea."

Ed grinned back at her but had to turn away. Her face glowed when she smiled, with the corners of her lips turned up, her eyes sparkling, reflecting the light from the sunshine that streamed in through the eastern window. Before he'd averted his gaze, he'd seen the gold flecks dancing around in those big brown eyes.

"I brought muffins," she told them. "Take a break and help yourself."

They all helped themselves, then returned to work. Jill followed Ed to the back, nibbling on the edge of a muffin, her eyebrows knit in a frown.

"You okay?" he asked.

"I guess," she said with a shrug.

Ed paused for a moment before he decided to take a leap and ask a question he knew could elicit either a cold stare or her fury—but he was willing to take a chance. "Would you like to go to our church sometime?"

She paused and stared at him for a moment. "Uh, maybe sometime."

"How about this Sunday?" he asked, looking directly at her.

Jill squirmed. "Not this Sunday."

"Why not?"

"I don't know, Ed. Maybe later, okay?"

"Sure, that's fine. I just figured you might want to visit our church. We have a lot of nice folks there, and the preacher has a great way of sharing the gospel."

"I think I'll just stick to reading my Bible for the time being. Back when my father was alive, he made me get all dressed up in stupid, stiff dresses he picked out for me. Then we had to sit quietly in hard, wooden pews while some preacher droned on and on about how bad we were. Then, when we got home, my father told me that if I didn't behave I'd burn in hell. I hated every minute of it." She paused and swallowed hard. "I know Jesus died on the cross for me, but I don't want to be miserable all the time feeling guilty."

That certainly explains a lot, Ed thought. He'd seen other Christians who worked the guilt angle on other believers, and he didn't like it, either.

"Did you ever listen to the message?" Ed asked.

A pained expression crossed her face. "Look, Ed—I'm not sure where you're going with this, but you're making me very uncomfortable. I read my Bible, and I'm a believer. You don't have to convert me."

"Yeah, I guess you're right." Time to step back.

"I'll find a church in my own time," she added. "Just don't rush me."

The bell on the front door jingled as a customer entered. "My break's over," Jill announced, jumping up to help the woman who was already perusing the shelves. "Go ahead and finish off the muffins. I'm done."

Ed sat there and stared after Jill, wondering what to do next. He didn't want to try to talk Jill into going to his church, but he did want her to come with him at least once. Even if she was getting the Lord's Word regularly through reading scripture, she still needed to worship somewhere.

❧

"Look, man. You gotta let go and let the Lord work through

you," Joe advised Ed later. The three men were sitting in the small café down the street eating sandwiches for lunch. "You can't force things."

Ed nodded. "I know."

Matt turned to Joe and snickered. "I think Jill's wormed her way into Ed's heart."

Not denying it, but also not admitting anything, Ed said, "As I already told you, Jill needs help in more ways than one, and I'm not a guy who shirks responsibility."

"Let's get back to work, then," Matt said as he stood up, pulled out his wallet, and dropped a couple of dollars on the table for the tip. "The little woman's waiting for us."

The shop was crowded when they got back, so the three men went right to work. Jill was constantly surrounded by customers, and she handled them beautifully. Ed again saw that she was in her element, which reinforced his resolve to help her as much as was humanly possible.

Several hours later Jill came back to see how he was doing. "Can I get you something?" she asked.

"Nah, I'm fine." Ed finished hammering in the nail and stopped, turning to face her. "Business is good today, huh?"

"Yeah, it's fair. I can't complain." She had a questioning look in her eyes, but she didn't ask anything.

"Look—I'm sorry if I upset you earlier."

"Upset me?" She tilted her head, forcing one huge lock of curls to flop out of her clip.

"About church. I didn't mean to bring up unpleasant memories."

"Don't worry about it. I'm okay." Her voice was tight, so he knew she wasn't okay. "I'm used to people trying to drag me to church. As soon as people find out I'm a Christian without a church home"—she snapped her fingers—"they start working on me."

That comment annoyed him. "I'm not trying to drag you to church, Jill."

"You weren't? Are you saying you don't want me to come to your church?" Now she was challenging him.

"Of course I want you to come to my church."

She grinned and let out a little chuckle. "Better make up your mind."

Now he realized she was teasing. Ed was grateful she'd finally relaxed around him.

As soon as she went back to her customer, Ed squeezed his eyes shut and prayed silently. *I'm ready to do Your will, Lord. Please show me how best to serve You and act according to Your plan. I want to do everything to Your glory and in Your timing.*

When he opened his eyes, Jill was staring at him, her eyebrows raised. "Sorry if I interrupted you," she said, "but I have a question about something upstairs."

four

After leading him upstairs, she stopped and turned to face him. "Well?" She pointed to a small shelf that lay on its side, shards of broken glass surrounding it.

"Looks like a mess."

Jill's frown deepened. "Yeah, it's a mess. We need to do something about it."

"Got a broom?" he asked.

She continued watching him. There was something in this picture he wasn't getting.

Finally he sucked in a deep breath and blew it out. "Okay, I give. Wanna clue me in?"

"You really don't know, do you? You have no idea."

"Right." Holding out his hands, he added, "I'm clueless, stupefied, and maybe downright ignorant."

"Seems to me like someone with your experience would understand what vibrations can do to glass."

"Vibrations? Glass?" He looked at the shards on the floor as it dawned on him. Pointing to the freestanding bookcase that had toppled over, he asked, "Did I do that?"

"Uh-huh. And that's not all. Look around."

He turned and scanned the room. Empty mirror and picture frames were scattered over the floor next to an interior wall. If his quick calculations were correct, that wall was directly above the one he'd been working on.

Doing a mental forehead slap, Ed offered what he hoped was a sincere look of contrition. "Look, Jill. I'm sorry. I'll replace it. All of it."

"How do you replace something that's irreplaceable?"

True. "Then I'll pay you for it. I'm truly sorry."

He saw her frustration, but there was nothing she could do or say, now that the damage was done. She lifted her hand to her face, covered her mouth, and shook her head as she glanced around the room.

"What can I do to make everything better, Jill?" he asked.

Her shoulders sagged. She had the look of a beaten-down woman with nowhere to go. Ed's heart lurched, but he refrained from wrapping his arms around her for comfort. He couldn't hold himself back completely, though. He took a step closer and gently placed his hand on her shoulder. She glanced up at him with an odd expression—one he couldn't read.

That was when he knew. "This has nothing to do with the broken glass, does it?"

She slowly shook her head and turned her back to him, placing another foot of distance between them. His heart ached for Jill. He wanted to help her, but he couldn't when she kept closing herself off to him.

"Jill? Please tell me what's troubling you."

Her body shook for a second before she spoke. "Just give me a minute, okay?"

He started to turn and head back downstairs, but he changed his mind. Bracing himself for whatever reaction she might have, he narrowed the gap between them and gently placed both hands on her shoulders. She suddenly stiffened.

"Jill," he said firmly.

She barely lifted her head an inch, but she didn't turn to face him. At least she didn't push him away.

"If you need me, I'm here. As for all this stuff I broke, I'll take care of it." Ed let go of her and backed away. "I was very careless." Then he walked away to give her some space.

He'd made it to the second step when he heard her voice.

"Ed," she said softly.

He paused and counted to three. When he spun around to face her, he hadn't expected to see her so close. Somehow she'd crossed the expansive room without his hearing her footsteps.

"Yes, Jill?"

"Thanks." She sniffled. "I'm sorry I went all nutso over the stuff that fell, but with all the stress. . ." She gestured around the room. "You know."

"Yes, I do know."

"And I know this isn't your fault. You had no way of knowing I had all this breakable stuff up here. I should have told you."

"I should have asked."

Ed's chest tightened as they stood there in silence. Years of being in control of every aspect of his own life and guarding his heart hadn't prepared him for this.

One thing he knew for certain: He couldn't continue walking on eggshells around her just to keep her from skittering away from him. He needed to be bolder and stand up for what he believed. Why should he back off just because he was dealing with a flustered woman? In fact, that was all the more reason he should be more aggressive.

Ed decided to take care of the problem at hand and figure out a way to witness to this broken woman. "Now, if you have a broom I'll clean this up."

"No, that's okay. I'll take care of it."

"I want—"

She gave him a dismissive wave of the hand. "No, that's okay, but thanks."

He had to force himself not to smile. With each word from her mouth came strength. *Atta girl.*

As Ed went back to work, he thought about what made Jill tick. Was she lonely? Or had something awful happened that made her so skittish? She'd told him a little about her dad, so perhaps there was more to it than what she'd said. Everyone needed someone, so he suspected she needed friends. He had his church friends, and he wanted to share them with her.

After Marcy's death he'd been lonely, too. And angry. Her gestational diabetes was supposed to go away after the babies were born. The unfairness of it all had nearly toppled his world. But his twin babies needed him, so he'd pushed his anger aside until eventually it just faded with time. And fortunately the church had been there for him when he needed them most—the very thing that solidified his faith that had been shaken to the core when Marcy died.

He'd actually stopped going to church for a while. But one of his subcontractors had persisted, and one of the elderly women from church came over to help care for the girls. With all that Christian love, he'd finally realized his faith was the most important aspect of his life.

He nearly slammed his hand with the hammer as he heard footsteps behind him. "Must be some good thoughts goin' on over there," Matt said.

"Hey, man, what's up? You finished with the wiring?"

"Not hardly." Matt hooked his fingers in his belt loops. "We've got a couple of issues here, and I need to talk to you for a minute."

"Shoot." Ed laid his hammer on the workbench. "What do you need?"

Matt gestured toward the back door. "Step outside?"

Dread washed over Ed. Taking it outside could only mean more bad news.

They'd barely stepped outside when Matt hit him with the news. "This place needs to be fumigated."

"Bugs?" Ed said with a nod. "Yeah, I did see a few."

"Yeah, there are bugs. Termites."

Ed groaned. "I saw 'em, too. Think it's bad enough to need tenting?"

"Positive. One of the walls is practically gone. Want me to talk to her?"

"No," Ed said. "Better not. Let's just handle it. I broke a few things, and that set her on edge, so I don't think she'd deal well with news of termites."

Matt nodded. "Okay, if you're sure. My wife comes home in a few days, so I need to get through this as quickly as I can and go back to my commercial job."

"Thanks, Matt."

Ed lingered in the backyard while Matt ambled back inside. Termite infestation. No doubt that would put Jill over the edge.

The door hadn't closed all the way when Ed saw Jill pushing on it. She was by his side in seconds.

"Taking a break?" she asked.

"Yeah, sort of."

He turned away, unable to face her. He wasn't going to lie to her, but he planned to wait until he figured out what to do before saying anything about the termites.

Clouds overhead floated between the earth and the sun, shading them for a few seconds. When the sun came back out, he noticed how it glistened on her hair, bringing out the copper highlights. She turned and smiled up at him.

"You're pretty when you smile," he said.

"Thank you." Her words were so soft they were barely a whisper.

❧

Jill had never wanted to kiss a man as much as she wanted to kiss Ed Mathis right this minute. His kindness radiated from his every pore. Just looking at him gave her a sense of security she hadn't had since her mother was alive.

She swallowed hard to try to get her voice back. "I really am sorry for overreacting about the broken glass. I guess I just don't deal with bad surprises very well."

"No one does, but unfortunately life has plenty of bad surprises."

"I've just had so many lately."

He smiled at her. "That's why I start and end my day with prayer."

Jill nodded and glanced away. She prayed, too, but she didn't like to discuss it. Her relationship with Jesus was very personal. When she'd talked to her father about it, he'd made her feel that her simple faith wasn't good enough, so she'd decided to keep some things to herself.

"I really appreciate all you're doing for me," she said, when she couldn't think of anything else to talk about.

"I think we've already established that. And I know you know I'm glad to do it."

She nodded. "Well, I guess I'd better get back inside, just in case I have another customer."

"Yeah, I guess you'd better."

She'd walked inside and barely rounded the corner when Matt greeted her. "Wiring will be done soon. I have to finish connecting the upstairs; then I'll disconnect the old wires. You should be in good shape—at least, electrically speaking."

Jill chuckled at his choice of words. "Thanks, Matt."

Grinning, he slapped his tool belt. "Glad to be able to help. Gotta get back to work." Then he disappeared, leaving her alone.

Jill had barely turned toward the register area when she heard Ed hollering from the backyard. She turned to the lone customer, said, "Be right back," and ran out to see what all the fuss was about.

"I see you've met Tiger." Jill looked down at the small yellow kitten standing at Ed's feet, her back arched and her fangs showing as she hissed up at him. She was so cute!

"He looks hungry," Ed said.

"She. And you're right. She's always hungry." She moved toward Ed, bent over, and scooped up the kitten before backing away from him.

"I didn't know you had a cat."

"I don't. She's a stray."

Ed frowned. "If you feed a stray cat, it becomes yours."

Jill shrugged. "How would I know? I never had a pet before. My dad wouldn't let me."

Ed's sympathetic expression unnerved her. She nuzzled the kitten to her cheek and rubbed her as she purred.

"I guess I'd better get back to finishing that wall," Ed said. "I'll leave you and your. . .Tiger to sort things out."

Once Ed had gone back inside, Jill carefully placed Tiger on the ground in front of her food bowl. Tiger glanced toward the door Ed had slammed behind him before turning her attention to the tuna morsels. "Looks like you and I are stuck with each other," Jill said softly to the kitten.

When Jill got back inside, Ed was working steadily on the wall. Without so much as turning around, he reached out. "I took care of your customer. She bought some little glass bowls, and I stuck the money in the envelope under the cash register. Mind handing me that spackling gun?"

"Uh, sure," she said as she glanced around and tried to figure out what he wanted. "As soon as you tell me what it is."

Ed chuckled as he pointed. "That big silver tube-shaped thing."

"Oh, that."

She stood and watched as he slowly and carefully finished off that section of wall, then cleaned up what little mess he'd made.

"Why are you so persnickety?" she asked.

"I like to do things right."

"Yes," she agreed, "but there are extremes."

He glared at her, so she quickly backed off. She was relieved to hear the bells jingle on the front door. "Want me to take care of this customer?" Ed joked.

She shot him a look as she ran to offer assistance. "Thanks a lot, but I'll get this one."

The woman who'd walked into the Junktique Shoppe had only stopped to ask directions.

"You should have seized the opportunity and sold her something," Ed chided.

She shrugged but didn't bother defending herself. What was the point? He had already obviously formed an opinion of how she conducted business, and it clearly wasn't a good one.

At the end of the day Jill headed home. She'd forgotten to open the blinds that morning, so the living room was dark. She found her way to the back of the long, narrow house. Everything was where she'd left it. As they did every day about this time, her father's words haunted her. Until she'd read the Bible on her own, her father had her convinced cleanliness was next to godliness. Now she knew he'd twisted scripture and used her ignorance against her. She was thankful for learning the gospel in college, or she wouldn't have understood the truth during this difficult time.

After a quick microwaved meal, Jill grabbed her collectibles book and headed for bed. She shut her eyes and asked God for His help getting through the next few months—or years—and eventually finding her way in the world. She had a hard time with prayer. She was never sure how to put her thoughts into a message Jesus would actually want to hear.

Thumbing through her collectibles book, Jill couldn't keep her mind on what she needed to do, so she shut her eyes to try to redirect her thoughts. She fell asleep with the book facedown over her chest and awoke to incessant chirping from a bird in the tree outside her bedroom window.

After cereal and coffee, she showered and dressed. She was about to leave for the day when she caught her reflection in the hall mirror. "Ugh." She did an about-face and headed back to her bathroom to put on some lipstick and a little mascara.

When Jill arrived in front of the shop, a half-dozen work vans and trucks were parked along the curb, barely leaving enough space for her car. They were mostly parked on one side of the street that was on a steep incline.

"Good morning, sunshine," Ed said when he saw her.

She swallowed hard and looked at him, then reached up to tuck a loose curl behind her ear.

"Don't," he said as he touched her hand. "I like the way the curl falls."

"I don't."

"Sorry." He turned to face a couple of his buddies who'd come out to ask him a question. "We only have a few more minutes before opening time. Almost done?"

They both nodded, then took their turns asking him about construction issues. Jill took advantage of his diverted attention and darted past them to go inside.

≈

Ed thought Jill was gorgeous before, but today she nearly left him speechless. One look at her, and he felt as if the wind had been knocked out of him. And her obvious vulnerability left him unable to run as far from her as he could and as fast as he knew he should. No way could he take off when someone obviously needed something from him.

He watched her for a little while before turning to his own work. He had to field a couple of questions, but he managed to finish a wall.

"Hey, Ed," she said as she approached him from behind. "Who's that man crawling around under the house?"

He spun around to face her. He had to spoon-feed her in bits and pieces, or she'd freak out. "Are you talking about the exterminator?"

She frowned. "Don't tell me I have bugs, too."

"Yeah, you do have some bugs."

Tilting her head to one side, she narrowed her gaze. "What's the big deal about bugs?"

"This house needs to be treated for pests," he said, trying hard to hold back anything that might trigger an alarm in her.

"Yeah, I guess you probably don't want bugs in your food when I start cooking dinner for you and your crew." She placed her fist on her hip and studied the floor for a moment before asking, "When do you want me to start?"

"Next week okay?" Ed asked. "I'll bring the food if you'll make a few extra servings for my girls."

Her face grew red. "I don't know anything about cooking kid food."

"My girls will eat anything you cook. In fact, we're going out to dinner tonight. Want to join us?"

She quickly shook her head. "No, thanks. I have. . .plans."

"Maybe some other time?"

"Uh, sure." He watched her process her thoughts before she said, "I'll start cooking on Monday if that's okay. I can cook at home and bring it in. I'll even make enough for Matt's wife and your children. I'd cook here, but I don't have a stove or a refrigerator in the kitchen yet."

"Oh, I almost forgot," he said. "Take a look at your kitchen."

"Wha—?" she said as she backed toward the kitchen, then turned and ran. A second later he heard her squeal. "Who brought the refrigerator? And why? There's no way I can pay for this."

"It's for the guys. You don't expect everyone to do all this work and not have a place to keep their soft drinks, do you?"

"But I don't—"

He held up his hands to quiet her. "Stop it right now, Jill. It's a little gift from all of us to the new shop owner in town. It's free."

Her eyes misted over, and he had to look away.

"I'm in the building business, Jill. We get special deals on appliances all the time. Really, it's no big deal."

"Nothing's free," she said hoarsely.

He wanted to remind her of the fact that salvation through Christ was free, but he didn't. He nodded and said, "It'll give us a place to keep the food you're cooking for us until we can get it home."

Jill looked around, desperation shrouding her features, until her eyes lit up. "Then how about letting me send you home with something from my shop? I know it isn't much, but there's bound to be something you might like."

Such pride. "Okay, how about something for my girls? Their room isn't exactly a designer's paradise."

Jill nodded. "Do they like bright colors?"

"Oh, yeah. The brighter the better. Blinding, in fact."

"I just picked up a box of stuff from an estate sale," she said as she sidestepped toward the storage area. She sounded excited. "The elderly woman must have had granddaughters because she had all kinds of kid things."

He glanced down at the box she was opening. It was full of. . .junk. "Would you mind picking out a few things a couple of little girls might like?"

Finally she smiled, showing off a glowing face and beautiful, soft, kissable lips he noticed were painted a pretty shade of peach. "Don't worry. I'll fix them right up."

"Remember—just a couple of things for each of them."

She grinned but didn't say a word as she rummaged through the box.

At the end of the day Jill had a couple of boxes crammed full of picture frames, toys, character clocks, and wall hangings. With a sly grin she shrugged. "Girls need their stuff."

He reluctantly carried one box to the truck while she followed behind with the other. "Thanks in advance from the girls."

All the way home he thought about how surprised the girls would be. They greeted him at the door as they always did. He crooked his finger and motioned for them to come out and help him carry in some stuff. As soon as they saw what was in the boxes, their eyes lit up.

"Oh, Daddy, this is so cool!"

They squealed with delight as they dug in, pulling things out of the boxes, tossing items to the side as they dug some more. He noticed how spartan the living room had been before and how these boxes of junk had livened up things so quickly. Maybe Jill had a point.

"Look!" Tracy said as she held up some bright red square thing he couldn't identify.

"What is it?" Stacy asked.

Tracy shrugged. "I don't know, but it's pretty."

Ed had to hide his laughter. Jill was right.

When they reached the bottom of the boxes, Stacy turned to him. "Tell that lady. . .Jill. . .we like it."

"Hey, how about some food?" he asked.

The girls ignored him. They were back into the pile of things and were staking their claim on what they wanted. In fact, they'd both decided they wanted something he couldn't identify, other than calling it "that round thing." He had to break up their argument by saying they could take turns picking what they wanted until everything was claimed.

"Just remember you have to put all this junk away when you're finished with it," he reminded them.

"It's not junk, Daddy," Stacy said. "It's cool stuff." She turned to her sister. "C'mon, Tracy—let's go eat and get it over with. Daddy won't let us play with this until we get back."

Throughout dinner the girls grilled him with questions about Jill and her shop. He answered their questions as they came at him rapid-fire.

Tracy suddenly grew quiet as she rested her chin on her fist and stared out the window of the restaurant. Stacy was still chatty as ever, so Ed had to interrupt.

"Whatcha thinking, Tracy?" he asked.

Tracy crinkled her forehead as she leaned forward. "Can Jill be our mommy?"

five

Okay, so maybe introducing his girls to Jill wouldn't be such a good idea. If something as simple as giving them a box of toys could get Tracy thinking like this, what would happen if they met?

"Tracy, honey. . ." He kicked his brain into high gear, trying his best to say the right thing. "Jill is just a friend. Why don't you simply enjoy her gift and leave it at that?"

She pouted. "But I want a mommy, and she's nice."

Stacy jabbed her. "How would you know if she's nice? We don't even know the lady."

Tracy turned to Ed. "Is she nice, Daddy?"

"She's very nice. But that doesn't mean she has to be your mommy. She can be our friend."

The rest of the night was spent discussing how they could do things with Jill as friends without making her their mommy. Ed had no idea what Jill would say, but that didn't matter at the moment. Besides, he didn't think she'd want to disappoint two very sweet little girls.

The next morning when he arrived at the shop he felt out of sorts. Jill had brought in some food, and she was sticking it in a microwave he hadn't seen before.

"Where'd you get that?" he asked.

Jill opened her mouth, but Matt stopped her. "I bought a new built-in for the house to surprise my wife, so I brought the freestanding one here for Jill."

"I offered to pay him," Jill said, "but he won't take it." She sighed. "So I'll just have to make breakfast, too."

Matt chuckled. "At this rate maybe you should have a café in the back of your shop."

"Now that's a thought," Jill said with a smile.

Suddenly Ed's day turned brighter—simply because Jill smiled. His heart melted at the warmth that lit up her face.

"I got a special deal on some prefab cabinets," Matt added. "One of the contractors I worked with on the last job had an extra set. They were dirt cheap, and I offered them to Jill. She's still trying to decide."

"Take them," Ed said. "You could use some cabinets."

Tension overtook Jill's face. "You said they were cheap, but you never did say how much."

"Practically free," Matt said as he glanced down.

Jill saw right through that. "I know they weren't free. Just give me a price."

"Pay me fifty dollars, and we'll be even," Matt said. "Hey, I gotta run. I have work to do. You can give me your answer later."

Ed was well aware the cabinets cost more than fifty dollars, but he wasn't about to interfere with his friend's generosity. Matt hadn't lied, but he sure had avoided Jill's question without giving a direct answer.

"Is fifty dollars too much?" Ed asked after Matt was gone.

She tilted her head and gave him a you've-got-to-be-kidding look. "I'm not stupid," she said.

"No, I realize that. But if Matt's offering you some cabinets for fifty bucks, you need to take him up on it."

"I hate being a charity case."

Ed decided to change the subject. "My girls loved their goodies. Thanks."

Jill offered a half smile. "I'm glad. You're very welcome."

"I never realized how something as simple as a box filled with trinkets would make them happy."

"I'm sure there are some things we both need to learn." The softness of her voice warmed his heart.

"Yes, I'm sure there are."

❧

The morning flew by for Jill. She had a steady stream of customers, most of them referrals from friends who'd been in before. People in Atlanta obviously loved antiques and collectibles. "This place is so charming," one woman said. "I hope you do well, dear."

Jill cut a glance over to Ed. She saw that he'd heard the woman, and that pleased her.

After the morning crowd thinned out, Ed stopped by the desk. "I'm going to lunch. Want something?"

"No, thanks. I brought a salad."

He offered a clipped nod. Once he was gone, Jill flopped into the chair beside the register desk. She was exhausted, and it wasn't just because she'd worked so hard all morning. Just being near Ed wore her out.

After giving herself a few minutes to recover, she headed back to the kitchen area that she hadn't seen since early morning. To her dismay, not only was the kitchen spotless, but a row of cabinets had been installed. She hadn't given Matt her final answer yet. Why wouldn't these guys let her make decisions for herself? Why did they assume they knew what was best for her?

She steamed and stewed until Ed returned from lunch. He took one look at her, dropped his smile, and took a step back. "Oh, no. What did I do now?"

Jill gestured around the kitchen. "Why, Ed?"

He shrugged. "I had to have someplace to put stuff, and they were right there in the back. It was easy, and I figured you couldn't pass up such a good deal."

As much as she hated to admit it, the kitchen was starting

to take shape. All she needed to make it a full, serviceable kitchen was a range. But she wasn't about to mention that, or she knew one would appear.

"Okay, I s'pose you're right. But from now on please give me time, and let me decide what I want in my shop. I'm a grown woman, and in spite of what you might be thinking, I'm responsible."

As soon as those words left her mouth, she realized what she'd said. Although she'd fought tooth and nail about being tied down, she really was a responsible adult. She wasn't nearly as flighty as her father had always made her feel.

Ed's expression was unreadable. Finally he nodded. "Yeah, you're right. I apologize. From now on you call the shots. Just tell me what to do, and I'll do it."

Jill groaned. "I didn't mean it like that. What I meant was—"

"That's okay. I understand. And I totally agree. This is your place. Matt and I have no right trying to muscle our opinions through. Want me to rip out those cabinets?"

"No, of course not. I know a great deal when I see one. I'm keeping them. I'll give Matt fifty dollars when he comes back."

⋇

Ed decided to tell Matt to cool it on his generosity since Jill would obviously bend over backward to repay them. They didn't need to add to her financial stress.

He went about his business while she assisted customers. Every time she entered the room where he was working, he had to fight the urge to watch her. Once, when she came back to get ceramic angels from the shelves he'd built, he found himself comparing her features to the angels'—and she won hands down.

Marcy had been softly pretty, too. But Marcy would never have ventured out on her own as Jill had. Then he remembered something important. Jill didn't exactly have a choice. Her mother had died when she was a child, and her father had died recently. She didn't have anyone, so she was stuck fending for herself. That very thought gripped his heart.

Ed had gradually started seeing more in Jill than her crusty exterior. She was soft inside, and he found her internal fortitude endearing. In fact, he admired how she not only pulled herself up to whatever she needed to do, but she also had a heart for her customers and seemed sincere when she offered her assistance.

That evening Stacy and Tracy greeted him with their chubby little arms open wide and expectant looks on their faces. "Sorry, girls. I didn't bring anything home today."

Tracy backed off, still pouting. Stacy, however, looked him squarely in the eye. "We wanted you to bring Jill home with you. Did you tell her you were making pancakes?"

"Pancakes are tomorrow night, squirt. Tonight's hamburger night."

She grinned. "Oh, then you can bring her home with you tomorrow night for pancakes. You make the bestest pancakes in the whole world."

Ed chuckled. "I'm not sure Jill even likes pancakes."

"Everyone likes pancakes," Stacy said with authority.

After dinner he read a story to the girls, then told them they could play for a few minutes before they got ready for bed. He went into the living room to pray and reflect.

His heartache over losing Marcy during their birth still hung over him, but the pain had dulled a little. Marcy had left such a wonderful part of herself behind in the girls. Although the girls were identical in looks, they had different personalities. Stacy was similar to her mother, all bubbly and lighthearted, with a touch of bossiness. Tracy was more like him—quiet and brooding with tendencies toward perfectionism and control.

Both girls were very intelligent and had similar interests. And to his utter delight they got along great, sticking up for each other no matter what.

A year after Marcy's death people in the church had started introducing him to women they thought would be perfect for him. But no one could ever take Marcy's place.

"Daddy!" The shrill voice snapped him from his trance.

"Huh? Something wrong?"

"We're thirsty," Stacy said. Tracy stood beside her, nodding.

He quickly stood, took them by the hands, and led them to the kitchen, where he got them each a glass of water. "Time for bed, girls."

After they put on their pajamas, he went to their room to hear their prayers. Tracy wouldn't let go of his hand when he stood to leave.

"Can we come to your work tomorrow?" she asked.

"No, I don't think that would be a good idea."

"Please?" Stacy begged.

"No." Ed went to the door. "Let's get some sleep." He heard them whispering as he walked to his room, and he knew they'd be up to something soon.

The next morning Ed was the first person to arrive at the Junktique Shoppe. Jill came in an hour later, laden with grocery bags.

By late morning his senses were accosted by the smell of Italian sauce. He dropped what he was doing and headed into the kitchen, where she stood over a two-burner hot plate, stirring sauce in a large pot. He'd have to hand it to her for ingenuity.

"Where'd you get the burner?" he asked.

"I had it in college. It was in a box in my spare bedroom." She stirred a few more times, then put on the lid. "Hungry?"

He grinned. "I am now."

Matt came walking in a few seconds later. "Something smells awesome."

By lunchtime Jill had a couple of tables cleared and plates lined up for a nice spaghetti lunch. She seemed pleased with herself as a half-dozen workers helped themselves to seconds, and some even had third helpings.

"Where'd you learn to cook like this?" Matt asked.

"I always cooked for my dad. He liked dinner on the table every night, and since I got home from school before he came home from work, that was my job."

Ed sensed that she hadn't particularly enjoyed cooking for her dad, but he knew she felt good about this. So he remained quiet as everyone else oohed and aahed over her fabulous culinary skills. She jumped up to assist customers when they walked into the store, so the workers used that time to nudge him. One of them even said, "She's a keeper, Ed. Better latch on to her." Ed quickly changed the subject.

Once everyone had finished, Ed helped Jill clean the kitchen. "Lunch was great," he said as he dried the last of the dishes. "I was wondering. . ." He looked at her as she turned to face him, her eyes wide. He had to swallow hard to continue. "I promised the girls I'd make pancakes for supper tonight. Would you like to join us?"

She fidgeted with her hair before shaking her head. "I don't think so," she said. "Not tonight."

Ed nodded and put the leftover spaghetti sauce in the refrigerator. Once everything was done, he returned to his project in the back room.

Every once in a while he heard the bell on the front door, but for most of the afternoon the place was quiet. He was startled when he glanced up and saw Jill staring at him.

"Need something?" he asked.

"I hate asking you to do this, but I have to run over to the bank. I'll only be gone a few minutes. Would you mind—?"

"Watching your shop?" he asked, finishing her question. He wanted to kick himself the instant he did it. It used to annoy Marcy to no end.

Jill grinned. "That's what I'm talking about."

She obviously didn't mind. He let out a sigh of relief. "I'll be glad to. Is everything priced?"

A look of amusement covered her face. "Yes, and I don't mind if you want to give a 20 percent discount. I've got it built into my prices."

"That won't be—." He stopped himself. "I'll do what I can."

"Thanks." She waved as she turned to leave.

Five minutes after she left, the place became swamped with business. And then, right after he closed the register after a large, multi-item sale in the hundreds of dollars, in walked Mrs. Cooper, the nanny, with his daughters on either side of her.

"Hey, Daddy!" Stacy said as she let go of Mrs. Cooper's hand and ran toward him. He bent down and scooped her into his arms while Tracy held on to the nanny's other hand and looked around the room.

"There's a lot of stuff in here," Tracy said in awe.

Flustered, Mrs. Cooper gently shoved Tracy toward him. "I hate to do this to you, Ed, but I have an emergency at home, and no one else from the church could cover for me."

"That's fine. In fact, I'll put them to work." *And maybe Jill won't freak out.*

In a matter of seconds, Ed found himself in Jill's shop with his daughters looking around, probably wondering what they could play with first. A brief panic filled him until he made a quick decision to knock off early and resume his work the next day. And he'd leave as soon as Jill returned from the bank.

A half hour passed, and Jill still hadn't arrived. Then another half hour went by. Ed had heated up some of the spaghetti for the girls, which killed a few minutes. But he could keep them out of trouble for only so long before he needed to do something.

Finally, an hour and a half later, she breezed in. She looked as if she was on the verge of apologizing when she suddenly stopped, looked at the girls, then glanced up at him, her mouth wide open.

"Daddy, is this Jill?" Stacy asked, breaking the silence.

"Jill, meet my daughters, Stacy and Tracy." He motioned toward Jill. "And this is Jill Hargrove. Mind if they call you Jill?"

Jill slowly shook her head, but she didn't utter a word. Both girls stared right back at her without speaking. Finally Ed knew something had to give. He turned to Jill.

"The nanny had an emergency, so she dropped them off here. I hope you don't mind, but I'm knocking off early."

"You don't have to do that," Jill said. "They'll be fine here."

Ed wished she hadn't said that in front of the girls, but obviously she didn't have much experience with children. Tracy tugged on his arm. "Can we, Daddy? Please?"

"Uh. . ."

Jill gestured around the shop. "I'm sure I can find something to keep them occupied while you finish your work for the day. It's the least I can do."

By this time Stacy had found the glassware and spotted a demitasse set. "Oh, look—some teacups."

Jill's eyes widened as she scurried to their side. "Hey, I've got something even better back here." She motioned for them to follow her to the back room, and they did. Ed was right behind them.

"Cool!" both girls said in unison.

Jill had pulled out a box filled with more colorful, girl-type trinkets. "This is more stuff from that same estate sale in Roswell," she explained. "You girls can have whatever you want."

"We can take it home with us?" Stacy asked.

Ed stepped up. "I have an idea. Why don't we keep it here for emergencies—at least until I've finished fixing everything."

Jill looked up at him, hesitated a second, then nodded. "That's fine."

Ed and Jill let the girls help them carry some of the things to the area where Ed had his workshop set up. "Hey, Jill, that b'sketti was good," Stacy blurted out. "Daddy said you cooked it."

"By the way," Ed said, "I fixed them some leftovers. I hope you don't mind."

"No, of course I don't mind," Jill replied. "I have some cookies in the cupboard."

The girls snapped their attention to Ed for approval. "Later," he said quickly.

Jill made a face and whispered, "Sorry. I never know what to say around kids."

"You're doing just fine," he replied. She was doing better than fine. He could tell the girls liked her.

Ed knew it was only a matter of time before they got curious and tried to wander, so he kept a close eye on them. To his surprise they stayed occupied for a couple of hours.

❧

Jill occasionally sneaked a peek back at Ed's daughters. They looked so much alike it was confusing—until one of them opened her mouth. Then she knew who was who. The quiet one was Tracy. They were both obviously smart, but they were different in how they showed it. Stacy made noise every time she moved. She suspected Tracy could be standing right behind her and she wouldn't even know it.

When the bell on the door sounded, she assisted a couple of

browsers who were just looking. They each bought something small, which was fine because Jill knew they'd be back. She was about to get some more merchandise to fill in the empty spaces when she heard a shuffling sound behind her.

"Jill?"

"Yes?" she said as she turned to face the little girl—the quiet one.

"Do you like our daddy?" The little girl stood there looking up at her with wide-eyed wonder.

six

Jill cleared her throat. "Why, uh, yes, of course I do."

Tracy tilted her head. "Then why won't you eat pancakes with us?"

"Um, I. . ."

Ed suddenly appeared. "Tracy, honey, Jill is a busy lady. I'm sure she has other things to do."

Tracy held out her hands. "But she has to eat, doesn't she?"

Both Tracy and Ed turned to her. He shrugged with an I-give-up look on his face. Jill didn't like being put on the spot, but how did she tell that to a four-year-old?

Finally Jill sighed. "Yes, I have to eat."

"Then come have pancakes with us," Stacy said from behind.

Was this normal behavior for four-year-olds? She wasn't sure, but they acted awfully old for their age.

"How old did you say you were?" Jill asked.

"Four," Tracy replied.

"Going on five," Stacy said, correcting her. "Our birthday is in a couple months."

"And we get to start kindergarten next year," Tracy added.

Well, that explained part of it. But still. . .

"How about it, Jill?" Ed said. "I flip a mean pancake, and the girls do have a point. You have to eat. I promise it won't take long."

"Okay, I'll go," Jill replied.

Ed and the girls stayed a little while longer until Stacy started whining. "Time for a nap," Ed said as he lifted one and took the other's hand. "I left our address and directions

70

by the register. We generally eat at six thirty, but come early if you can."

Jill nodded. What else could she do? She'd been ganged up on without a chance for defense. If it weren't for the children, she never would have agreed to go to their house.

She stayed at the shop until her posted closing time, then headed for the Mathis home in the Sandy Springs area. The neighborhood was older, but all the houses looked well maintained—especially Ed's place. Shrubs lined the front, with a row of annuals that hadn't given in to the cooler weather of autumn. She parked her car and said a short prayer that she wouldn't say something stupid as she headed up the sidewalk. She wasn't halfway to the porch when the front door swung open and both girls came bounding out of the house, nearly throwing themselves at her. She felt her heart flutter quickly.

Ed seemed as comfortable in his kitchen as he was at work. She was amazed at how orderly his home was, considering he had a couple of small children to deal with. And the pancakes were incredible!

"These are good," she said as she mopped up the blueberry syrup with the last bite.

"Want more?" Ed asked, obviously pleased with himself.

She held up both hands. "I'd love more, but I'm so stuffed I feel like I might pop."

Both girls doubled over in fits of giggles. "Don't pop, Jill!" Stacy said. "That would be gross."

Ed winked at Jill before turning to the girls. "Okay, kiddos, go play in your room for a few minutes. I want to chat with Jill before she leaves."

To her surprise they did as they were told. Jill turned to Ed. "You're doing a great job with them."

He pursed his lips and shook his head. "Thanks, but I'm

afraid they might be missing some things without their mother here."

Jill had no idea what to say to that, so she carried her plate to the sink. "Let me help you clean up; then I have to go."

He took the plate and led her away from the kitchen. "I have the rest of the night to clean the kitchen. Why don't we go to the living room and talk?"

Jill was relieved Ed sat on the sofa across from the chair she'd chosen. Once they started chatting, she felt as if she'd known him all her life.

After a half hour of relaxing small talk, Jill stood. "I really need to go. Should I go say bye to the girls?"

Ed paused, a contemplative look on his face, then shook his head. "They might try to find a way to keep you here longer."

Jill laughed as she took a step toward the front door. "You have two very smart little girls."

"I'll walk you to the door before the girls come out and expect you to entertain them."

"Thanks for everything, Ed. The pancakes were wonderful. The girls are sweet, too."

All the way home she thought of how good Ed was with his girls. They were cute and sweet, but they were also a handful. And Ed was charming and fun.

That night Jill lay in bed rehashing the events of the day. She'd had more than her share of surprises. Meeting Ed had brought something into her life she'd never experienced before—a sense of community. Then she had to remind herself it was only temporary—that he'd soon be gone.

The next morning she took her time getting ready. When she arrived at the shop, she saw Ed had gotten there first and let himself in. He was waiting on a customer. She was about to take over when she heard the elderly woman's response to him. "You're such a sweet boy for showing me all those cookie jars."

"You said you collect them, so it was the least I could do." He gave Jill a wink and a wave.

The woman turned around and spotted Jill. "Is that your wife?"

Ed coughed, and Jill felt like hiding. He quickly recovered. "No, I'm just helping her out for a while until she gets everything settled. Did you want all of the cookie jars?"

The woman nodded. "Yes, dear. How can I pass up such a wonderful deal by such a charming young man?"

After she left, Jill glared at Ed. "Why didn't you wait for me?"

He looked at her sheepishly. "I'd just let myself in to do my work, and she followed me inside. I didn't want to risk having you lose business."

"What kind of deal did you give her? Twenty percent off?"

He shook his head. "No, all I told her was that they were a good value individually, but as a collection they were worth quite a bit more."

"How did you know that?"

He pointed to the book by the cash register. "She came in and looked at them first thing. While she was walking around the store, I looked them up in your book. I hope you don't mind."

"No, of course I don't mind." Ed's kindness touched her heart, but she didn't know how to tell him.

"I was starting to wonder."

Jill leaned over and glanced around him. "Where are the girls?"

"The nanny's back—at least for the time being. Her daughter's due to deliver in about a month."

He turned and went back to his work area, leaving her alone in the front of the shop. Lunchtime came and went without incident. The shop was busy all afternoon, so time passed quickly. Jill glanced up as Ed appeared shortly before she'd planned to leave.

"See ya tomorrow," he said with a wave. He hesitated before he left. Jill stared after him, wondering what would happen once he and his friends finished their work. She'd long since given up the notion of letting him go and bringing in someone else to do the work. She trusted Ed, and the more she came to know him, the more she wanted him around.

❧

Ed knew he needed to get an early start the next morning because Mrs. Cooper was starting to make sounds about her daughter needing her very soon. He asked a neighbor to come in until Mrs. Cooper arrived.

He'd fully expected to be at the shop before Jill, but to his surprise her car was parked in front when he pulled up behind her. He walked in to find her moving some of the stock from the back room.

"Do wonders ever cease?" He grinned.

She glanced up. "What are you talking about?"

"You're actually early today."

She tightened her jaw but didn't say anything. He could tell he'd annoyed her. Oh, well. He was here to do a job.

The shop phone rang, but he ignored it until Jill appeared. "It's for you," she said.

With a frown he took it. Mrs. Cooper told him she needed to drop off the girls because her son-in-law had just called and was taking her daughter to the hospital.

Jill remained standing there, staring at him. When he clicked the OFF button and handed the phone back to her, she took it but didn't budge.

"Well?" she said. "Is there a problem at home?"

"No, not a problem. Just that Mrs. Cooper is bringing the girls here, and I'm nowhere near finished."

"That's fine," Jill said. "We have that box of toys they can play with."

"But you've been around them enough to know that'll only be good for a little while."

She grinned. "Then I suggest you get movin' on whatever project you're working on now."

"Yes, ma'am."

"Smart man." Jill pulled away from her spot leaning against the doorframe. "I'll let you know when they arrive."

Ed didn't need anyone to tell him when his girls arrived. Between Mrs. Cooper's loud, husky voice and Stacy's shrill bossiness, he knew the moment they walked in the door.

"Don't you girls touch a thing," Mrs. Cooper barked. "This store has a lot of breakables."

He put down his hammer and ambled out to the front of the shop where Mrs. Cooper chatted with Jill. Stacy and Tracy had wandered over toward the stairs. He rushed over to the twins, took them by the hand, and led them away.

"But I wanna go upstairs."

"Not now. I have to finish my work; then maybe I can take you."

Stacy broke free of his grasp and ran over to Jill. "Jill, can you take me upstairs?"

Mrs. Cooper glared down at her. "Now what did I tell you on the way over here?"

Stacy planted her little fist on her hip. "Miss Hargrove's store is filled with priceless antiques. She won't like you if you break anything."

Jill gasped as she turned to Mrs. Cooper. Ed understood his daughter had probably left out something. But Jill obviously didn't know that.

"I'm sure Mrs. Cooper didn't say it exactly like that," Ed said.

"I certainly didn't," Mrs. Cooper agreed. "I told her Miss Hargrove would be very unhappy if the girls broke something."

Ed noticed Jill's relief. "That's what I thought," he said. "Jill, would you mind taking one of the girls up for just a minute? I'd like to have a word with Mrs. Cooper before she leaves."

"I can take both of them," Jill said.

Ed and Mrs. Cooper simultaneously said, "No!"

Jill took a step back. "Well, in that case. . ." Jill glanced back and forth between the girls, obviously trying to decide which girl to take.

"Stacy," Ed said, "why don't you go first? I'll take Tracy up when I'm finished with Mrs. Cooper."

That satisfied Stacy. She marched right up to Jill, held out her hand, and led the way to the stairs. Jill glanced over her shoulder with another look of helplessness as she went with Stacy. Ed saw her vulnerability, and it flipped his heart once again.

After Mrs. Cooper apologized and said she had no idea when she'd be back to help with the girls, Ed realized how much denial he'd been in. He'd known for months she was planning to do this, but until now it hadn't seemed real. It was difficult to find substitute nannies for a day or two, but for an indefinite period of time? That would be next to impossible.

By the time Ed and Tracy joined Jill and his other daughter upstairs, he figured Stacy would have long since worn out her welcome. Instead he was pleasantly surprised by the sight of Jill showing Stacy some very tiny figurines in a corner beside a dollhouse. Stacy was actually behaving herself.

"Hey, you two," he said to let them know he was there. "Must be good to have both of you so interested."

Jill glanced up. "I was just showing her some fifty-year-old porcelain pieces."

Tracy tugged at him to take her closer, so he complied.

When he was close, he carefully let go of Tracy's hand so she could see.

Finally, after the girls looked over everything that interested them on the second floor, Ed led them back downstairs. Jill was right behind them.

She remained in the front of the shop while he situated them beside his work area. Then he came up to thank her.

"I appreciate your understanding. Not everyone can handle my girls."

Jill tilted her head to one side. "I don't know why you're so appreciative when you're the one doing me a favor."

"Well, I—"

"Besides," she interrupted, "your girls are really sweet. I don't see a single problem with either of them."

"They have their moments," he mumbled.

"Daddy!" Tracy hollered.

That caught both his and Jill's attention. They went running back.

Tracy was standing on a chair, pointing at a cornered and frightened Tiger. "Look at the kitten!"

Somehow Tiger had slipped into the shop and stood shivering in the corner of the back room, obviously frightened by the noise. "That's Tiger," Ed said. "Be very gentle with her. She's just a kitten."

"Can we play with her?" Stacy asked as she reached down to touch the animal.

"Very carefully," Ed answered.

While the girls were busy with the kitten, Ed told Jill he had something to discuss with her. Seeing the kitten reminded him she had termites.

The exterminator had told them the place was so heavily infested with termites that there was no way around tenting it. Then, after the tent came down, some of the flooring and walls needed to be replaced.

"What?" Jill asked.

With the girls right there and Jill looking tense, he decided to wait one more day. He wanted to finish his job at hand and discuss the severity of the problem with Jill when they were both able to talk.

"Can you be here early in the morning?" Ed asked.

Jill cocked her head to one side. "Like what time?"

"How about nine?"

She thought about it then nodded. "Nine is okay. I'll be here then."

"Good," he said. "Now let me get back to my work, so I can take the girls home before they get rowdy."

Fortunately the kitten kept the girls busy long enough for him to finish what he was doing. In fact, he had to drag them away when it was time to leave. Jill waved as they left.

All night the girls chattered about how much they loved kittens. "Daddy, please can we have a kitten or puppy?" Stacy asked.

"Not now, sweetheart," he replied. "Maybe someday when you're older."

"Why not now?" Stacy said, scowling.

"I want you to be old enough to take care of an animal. You have to feed them and make sure all their needs are met."

"We can do that."

Ed sighed. "Not now, girls. Let's get supper so we can go to bed at a decent time."

The girls struggled with him for a little while, but finally they calmed down and did what he told them to do. He figured they were eager to conspire.

As soon as he had tucked them in, he grabbed his phone and punched in the number of his exterminator. "Hey, Ray, I need you to go to the Junktique Shoppe first thing in the morning.

I'm ready to get an estimate for the fumigation."

Ray chuckled. "Okay, what time do you want me there?"

"She'll be there at nine, so I thought maybe you and I could meet at eight. Will that be enough time?"

"Sure thing," Ray said. "I'll see you then."

Early the next morning the neighbor, Mrs. McKnight, agreed to come over as long as the girls were asleep. She liked the girls, but two of them had been too much for her to handle the few times she'd tried to babysit them.

Ed thanked her again and took off, hoping to arrive at the shop before Jill. *Uh-oh*, he thought as he turned onto the street. He glanced at his watch and saw that it was a quarter to eight, and both Jill and Ray were parked in front of the shop.

He ran inside the shop, but neither Jill nor Ray was there. One glance out the back window, and he spotted them. He made his way through the back door as fast as he could.

Just as he thought. He saw frustration written all over her face.

"How long have you known how bad it was?" Jill asked.

Ed shuffled his feet. "Awhile."

She gave him a look of disbelief. "And when did you plan to tell me?"

"Soon."

Her cheeks puffed as she blew out a breath, pulled away from him, and started pacing in the backyard. "I don't know what to do."

"The place needs to be tented."

Ray nodded. "That's the only way. I told Ed—"

"I'm doomed," she said. "It seems like there's no end to what's wrong with this place."

Ed tried to think quickly of a solution, but he couldn't. All he could think about was how closing her doors long enough for the exterminator to fumigate the building could put her out of business. Since Ray was giving such a discounted rate, they couldn't very well rush him. He was working it in between jobs. Ed had a warehouse she could use while the place was fumigated and repaired, but he had a feeling she wouldn't go for it.

"I have a plan that'll be a hassle, but it just might work," he said.

Both Ray and Jill turned to him. He shot Ray a glance, so Ray excused himself, saying he had to look around a bit more and do some measuring.

After Ed told her about his warehouse, she shook her head. "How are we going to get all this stuff to your warehouse and back? There's no way. Besides, I can't take another handout from you."

"Do you have any other ideas?" he asked. "If you want, you can rent the space while you're there."

She frowned and set her jaw as she thought about it. Then slowly she shook her head. "I'm sunk."

"Maybe not. I can call some people from the church and—"

She held up her hands. "I don't think so. I don't know any of those people. Why would they want to help a complete stranger?"

"Because they're nice people, and they want to do what the Lord calls them to do," he said.

Jill obviously didn't know what to say. She just stood there staring off into the distance.

After a long silence Ed finally said, "Well? What do you think about me calling some of my friends?"

She kicked the ground in frustration. "Do I have a choice?" She paused, then added, "And don't forget I'll pay you rent for the time I'm there."

"Jill, you always have a choice. I'm not being bossy."

"No, I realize that. It's just that. . .everything's so overwhelming right now. I had no idea running a shop would require so much work. It's almost as bad as having a kid." The instant those words left her mouth, her eyes widened. "I didn't mean it like that." She flapped her arms by her sides, then shook her head. "I'm sorry, Ed. Your girls are wonderful. You're a great dad."

Ed felt sorry for her. She thought she'd insulted him, when in an odd sort of way she'd just given him a huge compliment. She'd let him know she was aware of the responsibility of having kids. But what she didn't seem to realize was that having a business wasn't exactly an irresponsible endeavor, either.

"You'd probably make a wonderful mother if you ever wanted kids," Ed said. "In the meantime we need to take care of this little problem."

She chuckled. "Little problem? I'm sorry, but I don't see how having termites is a *little* problem. It's pretty major to me."

"You know what my offer is, so let me know soon."

Ed backed off to let her process the news. The timing was good because Ray had come from the other side of the building. He motioned for Ed.

"Seeing's how you're trying to help this lady out and I'm not all that busy at the moment. . .if we can get moving on this by the end of the month, I can do this for half my regular fee."

Ed squinted. "Are you sure, Ray? I'm not asking for a discount."

Ray nodded. "If I can't do this for a helpless woman, what kind of man am I?"

Ed couldn't help but laugh at Ray's choice of words. "You're a good, honest, hardworking Christian man."

Ray squared his shoulders. "If I could do this for nothing I would, but I have to hire help to put up the tent and all. . . ."

"Hey, that's fine," Ed said. "I understand. Just do me a favor and don't tell Jill how much this is gonna cost. I'm taking care of it."

Ray grinned. "You're sweet on this girl, aren't you?"

Ed gulped. He'd been avoiding his feelings for Jill, but Ray was right. He didn't have to admit it, though. "We're friends, if that's what you mean."

"Okay, whatever you say. Call me tonight, and I'll get started as soon as you give me the go-ahead."

"I have to arrange for some people to help move her stuff."

Ray gestured toward his own truck. "I can help, too."

"Thanks." Ed extended his hand, and Ray shook it then left.

"What was all that about?" Jill said from behind.

"We need to talk about when to do this," Ed said.

"Whenever you want to is fine with me."

"Good. I'll make some calls, and we'll get it taken care of right away."

"Now, is it safe for me to go back inside?" Jill asked.

Ed chuckled. "You'll be fine."

The phone in Ed's pocket vibrated. He figured it was the babysitter begging to be rescued.

He explained to Jill that he might not be back for the rest of the day. A panicked look crossed her face, but she recovered in a split second. "That's okay. Do whatever you have to do."

After he got home and relieved his neighbor of childcare responsibilities, he called the Junktique Shoppe. No one answered. Jill must have a customer, he figured.

"Come on, girls. Brush your teeth and get dressed."

"Do we hafta?" Stacy whined.

"Yep," he said. "That is, if you wanna go see Jill."

"C'mon, Tracy. Let's do what Daddy says."

seven

When they arrived at the shop, the door was locked, and Jill was nowhere to be found. "Where is she, Daddy?" Stacy asked.

"I can't imagine." He led the girls around to the back of the house, thinking she might be in the backyard. She wasn't.

"Tell you what. I have a key, so we can go inside. I have a bunch of work to finish, so you girls can play with the toys Jill set aside for you."

Stacy looked at Tracy, who sighed. He could tell they were up to something.

They'd barely gone inside and turned on the lights when a couple of elderly women came in. "We heard about this place," the taller of the two women said. "Mind if we take a look around?"

"Be my guest," he replied. "The owner isn't in at the moment, but if you need something I'll try to help you."

While they browsed, Ed settled the girls on a small braided rug in the back room with the box of colorful items between them. That ought to keep them occupied for at least an hour or two, he figured. After that he'd have to come up with something different.

About fifteen minutes later one of the women stuck her head around the corner. "We'd like to buy a few things. Can you ring us up, or do we need to come back later?"

Ed set his hammer on the floor and wiped his hands on the rag he kept by the sawhorse. "I'll do it. Give me just a minute." Once the woman went back into the shop, he bent over and instructed the girls to stay right where they were. "Don't move off this rug until I come back. Got that?"

They both nodded before they exchanged a glance. He shot them a warning look before going to the sales area to help the ladies.

The women were barely out of the door when Jill came running into the shop, out of breath. "What are you doing here?" she asked.

He lifted his eyebrow as he widened his stance and folded his arms across his chest. "The question is, where were you? You had customers."

"What did you sell them?"

He shook his head. "I can't remember everything. . . . Let's see." He shut his eyes for a moment to get a visual picture of everything on the counter as he rang it up. "A couple of parchment lamp shades, some salt and pepper shakers, and a couple of bowls from upstairs. There was other stuff, too." He tried to think of the rest of it, but there was too much. He shrugged and added, "A bunch of stuff."

By that time Jill had her cash drawer open, and she'd pulled out the checks the women wrote. "Is this what they paid?"

He nodded. "If it's not right, I'll make up the difference."

Jill gave him an odd look. "I just hope they come back. They paid a lot of money."

Ed laughed out loud. "I think those ladies will come back. In fact, they were talking about bringing their whole bridge group. I told them you were temporarily relocating, and they said it didn't matter where you were; they'd find you."

Jill slowly grinned at him. That warmed him from the inside out. He could tell she'd softened toward him, and that made him feel good.

"Now, if you don't mind, I need to get back to work. The girls have been a little too quiet, and I have a feeling my time here today is limited."

"Be my guest," she said with a dismissive wave of her hand.

৵

Ed's attitude toward her shop baffled her. He clearly didn't understand how much her "junk" meant to people; yet he seemed so eager to help. His kindness and gentle spirit had touched her deeply. He'd started to chip away at the shell she'd formed around her heart.

But something bothered her. How did he do all the things he did? Her lack of confidence only deepened when she was around people like Ed. Not only did he have his job and his girls, but he jumped in and took care of her shop while she ran home to turn off the coffeepot she'd forgotten that morning in her haste to get to the shop early. She had been right in the middle of ringing up her first customer when it had dawned on her.

She could hear Ed in the back, alternating between hammering, sawing, and chatting with his daughters. An odd, warm sensation traveled through her as she imagined what it would be like to have a nice, cozy family like that.

Matt came walking in shortly after lunch, sporting a wide grin. "My wife was pleased as punch when I told her I was bringing home dinner tonight. Whatcha cookin'?"

Panic rose in her chest as she realized she'd forgotten all about dinner. She was about to say the first thing that came to mind when Ed snuck up behind her. "How about some steaks?"

Jill spun around and saw the look of amusement on his face. "Steaks?"

"Yeah," he replied. "I bought a bunch last week. I figured I'd bring them over."

"But I thought—," Matt began before Jill turned back to face him.

Jill made a quick decision. "Never mind Ed's steaks. I'm cooking Swiss steak."

"Yum," Matt said, patting his belly.

Suddenly she thought about the girls. "Do Stacy and Tracy like Swiss steak?"

Ed shrugged. "I dunno. They've never had it."

"Maybe I should fix something else."

"No, if you want to cook Swiss steak, then do it. If they don't like it, we have plenty of peanut butter at home."

"We love Swiss steak!" screeched Stacy as she came running full steam out of the back room.

"How would you know, squirt?" Ed bent over and scooped her up in one move. He started tickling her until she nearly choked on her giggles.

"Seriously, I can cook whatever they like."

Matt made a puppy-dog face. "But I had my heart set on Swiss steak."

Ed laughed. "You just like to eat, Matt."

Matt stuffed his hands in his pockets. "True."

After Matt left, Jill asked Ed to keep an eye on the shop again for a little while. He lifted his eyebrow.

"Are you sure you trust me with your precious shop?" he asked.

Jill snickered. "I'll be back as soon as possible."

"Take your time. I want you to catch me waiting on your customers."

As soon as Jill stepped in her car, she turned the radio dial to the local Christian station. She'd heard it recently blaring from Ed's truck, and she thought about how she needed to fill her mind and heart with uplifting messages and music. She could tell Ed wanted to discuss faith because he'd touched on it several times but backed off when she'd reacted. She knew she needed to be more open, but she hated people trying to coerce her into doing something she didn't want to do. And she wasn't into attending a church where people would judge her or anything about her.

The roads were crowded with cars and service trucks, as they always were during the workweek in Atlanta. Her trip to the grocery store took a little longer than she'd planned, but she managed to get through the express line and out in record time.

She was back at the shop less than an hour later. Ed stood at the counter ringing up another customer, and the girls were busy charming the elderly woman making the purchase.

When the woman spotted Jill, she grinned. "Your little girls are so precious. I miss my grandchildren."

Jill started to correct the woman and let her know they weren't hers, but Ed interrupted. "Thank you, Mrs. Bennett. I hope you enjoy your dolls."

"Oh, I will," she said as she took the bag and made her way to the door. "And I'll be back after the move." She wiggled her fingers toward the girls, and they waved back.

"If you know her, how come she didn't know I wasn't their mother?" Jill asked.

"Oh, I didn't know her until today. I got her name off her check."

"I see," Jill said. "Let me put this stuff in the refrigerator, and I'll be right back to relieve you."

"Take your time. I'm having fun."

She snapped around to see if he was serious, but she couldn't tell. His eyes twinkled with mischief. At least by now she trusted him enough to know he wasn't doing anything to muddle up her business.

The second she opened the refrigerator door to put the food away, Stacy was by her side. "My daddy likes you," she said.

Jill felt flustered. "He's a nice man."

"Tracy and I like you, too."

Now Jill felt more comfortable since this was between her and Stacy rather than Ed. She bent over, gently cupped Stacy's chin in her hand, and looked her in the eye. "I like you and Tracy very much."

Stacy's eyebrows shot up, and a wide grin flashed on her face. "You do?"

"Yes. You and Tracy are two of the sweetest little girls I've ever met. And the smartest, too."

Suddenly Stacy's smile turned into a frown. "My daddy's sweet. Why didn't you tell me you thought my daddy was sweet and smart?"

Jill tried to dig deep to come up with an answer. She was about to say something that probably wouldn't make sense to an almost-five-year-old when Ed saved her.

"Stacy, come on—let's go," he said from the doorway. "Jill needs to get back to work." He looked Jill in the eye and added, "The pastor's wife has agreed to watch them for a couple of hours this afternoon, so I'll be back."

Jill simply nodded because she was speechless. After Ed left, she leaned against the wall and rubbed the back of her neck. She never realized how draining children could be or how they could make her smile.

Before meeting Ed and the twins, all she had to deal with was the latent anger she wasn't aware of until after her father passed away. At least that was something she could understand. Her feelings for Ed, Stacy, and Tracy were confusing. Her defensiveness toward Ed was fading quickly, and she'd begun to feel more than just a physical attraction toward him. He didn't simply talk about his faith. He lived it. The differences between Ed and her father were becoming clearer to her by the day.

She managed to get dinner cooked between customers. The two-burner hot plate was challenging, but at least she had that until she could afford a full-size range.

Ed came back after she'd put dinner in the refrigerator in individual pans ready for the guys to take home. He sniffed the air and smiled.

"Smells wonderful in here," he said. "Just like I imagine a home should smell."

Jill forced a smile. That was an odd thing for him to say. What did he mean by that?

Ed headed straight to his work area and started hammering. She knew his time was limited, so she didn't want to bother him. But later they needed to talk.

Matt stopped by and picked up his meal. "I appreciate this," he said. "But don't think you have to do it every day. In fact, I won't be by tomorrow or the next day."

"Then just let me know when you'll be back," she offered. "It's important for me to do this."

He smiled and offered a slight nod. "I understand. I'm the same way." He leaned over to look at Ed, then lowered his voice. "So's Ed, but he won't admit it."

Jill offered a conspiratorial smile. "Yes, I know. Thanks for all your help, Matt."

So far Jill had liked everyone she'd met from Ed's church. Every last one of them was open and giving, although they had completely different personalities. Rather than clashing, though, they seemed to complement each other. They had a spirit of community about them, and she'd discovered she liked the feeling of being part of it—even if she was an outsider reaping the benefits simply because Ed had put it upon himself to take care of her.

As she closed out her cash register, Ed appeared. "By the way, I've lined up a bunch of people and their trucks to move you this weekend."

Jill stifled the urge to give him another chance to back down. "Fine. I'm not sure what a move like this involves—"

"It's a lot of hard work, but it'll only take a day with all the people we'll have working."

৯৯

What Ed didn't tell her was that he'd been building shelves and getting the front part of his warehouse ready for her to move right in. He'd even taken some carpet remnants and covered the showroom floor, which would help quite a bit to prevent breakage of some of her more fragile items.

"One of these days I want to do something for every single person who helps," she said softly.

Ed fully understood. He'd always had a hard time accepting anyone's help—that is, until Marcy died. When that happened he'd gone around in a state of numbness. After he finally pulled out of it, he realized the only thing that had gotten him through it was the Lord's hand in bringing the generosity of the church people to his aid. Now it was Jill's turn to accept the same thing.

"Are you ready to leave yet?" she asked as she stood poised at the door, keys in hand.

"No, you go right ahead," he replied. "I'll lock up when I leave."

"Don't forget your dinner," she reminded him. "It's on the top shelf of the refrigerator."

"Trust me—I won't forget."

Out of the corner of his eye, he saw her watching him for a moment before she finally left. He stood there and stared at his handiwork as he thought about what lay ahead of them. If she had any idea of the magnitude of the problems she had, she would likely give up and disappear from his life.

He finally admitted his instant attraction and growing affection for Jill. Her warmth and kindness toward her customers showed her innate goodness. It hadn't taken him long to see through her gruff exterior. She'd been badly hurt in the past, so that was understandable. What he now saw in her was the desire to succeed in her lifelong dream while bringing joy to others. He found this even more attractive than her physical appearance. His girls clearly liked her, too, which would make it difficult when the time came to move on. He couldn't expect Jill to take on a relationship with a man and two small kids after she'd made it clear she didn't like responsibility.

The irony of the whole situation was so obvious it was painful. Jill talked about how she shirked responsibility; yet she had plenty with this shop. He'd agreed to do light handyman work while taking a break before embarking on what he knew would be a long-term project with the residential and commercial community he'd proposed. They both wound up with surprises.

When he picked up the girls, the pastor's wife, Emma Travers, offered to watch them again the next day. "I understand how hard it must be to work with them underfoot. I have to run a couple of errands, but I can take them with me."

He smiled and thanked her.

"And since you'll be here for the potluck and Bible study tomorrow night, just come straight here from the shop."

That night the girls giggled about the things they'd done at the pastor's house. "When Pastor Travers walked in, we surprised him," Stacy said.

"What did you do to surprise him?" Ed asked.

"We yelled 'boo!'" Both girls fell into giggles.

"I hope you didn't scare him too much," Ed said, pretending to be shocked.

Tracy tilted her little head forward, allowing her honey-colored curls to bob around her face. "Daddy, this is the pastor we're talking about. He's not scared of nothing."

"Anything," Stacy corrected.

"He's not scared of anything," Tracy said. "He knows he has Jesus there with him, and two little girls *can't hurt him*."

Maybe not, Ed thought, *but two little girls sure can scare Jill*.

The next morning Ed dropped the girls at the parsonage,

thanked Emma profusely, and then headed back to the shop. Jill had brought in some boxes, and she'd already packed half of one row of shelves, with dozens more to go.

"This is going to take forever," she said.

"Just wait until my friends arrive. We'll have this place packed up in no time."

Jill pressed her lips together, then went back to wrapping some fragile glass. Ed wanted to step in and help, but she looked just as fragile as the collectibles.

All day he felt as if he were walking on eggshells around Jill. She was in a strange mood. Every move she made seemed tentative, almost as if she wasn't quite sure what to do next.

Shortly after lunch, she told Ed she needed to start dinner. He'd forgotten to tell her about the weekly church dinner, so he explained it to her now. "You're welcome to join us," he said.

She shook her head without a moment's hesitation. "No, thanks. I'll just go home. I'm pretty tired."

Ed instantly felt bad because he knew it seemed like an afterthought to invite her. If someone had asked him under the same circumstances, he would have turned them down, as well. He made a mental note to keep trying, but not to wait until the last minute.

A few minutes after Jill drove away, he left the Junktique Shoppe and headed for the church, making one quick stop at a bakery on the way. The girls were playing in the parsonage yard when he pulled into the church parking lot. The instant they spotted him, they took off after him, squealing in delight. Emma Travers followed right behind them, telling them to wait until he stopped the truck.

"Daddy, Daddy! Guess what! There's a stray cat at the church. Mrs. Travers says we can have her if it's okay with you."

"What?" he said as he turned his focus to the woman coming

up behind the girls. "Did you say that?"

She shook her head, a smile playing on her lips. "Not exactly in those words."

Ed sighed as he lifted the bakery box from the passenger seat of the truck. "Let me think about it, girls. In the meantime let's get you settled inside. I brought brownies for the potluck."

Stacy jumped up and down beside him. "Can I have a brownie now, Daddy? Please? If I promise to eat all my supper?"

Before Ed could say a word, Tracy shook her head. "You know Daddy's not gonna let us have a brownie now. You have to eat your supper *first*."

"That's right," Ed agreed as he opened the door with one hand and ushered his daughters inside while balancing the box of brownies with the other.

He helped the girls fill their plates with the healthiest food he knew they'd eat. Then he found them a spot at one of the long tables before he went back to get his own food. Emma was at the next table, pouring a glass of tea.

"Here ya go, Ed," she said as she came around and handed it to him. "I want to apologize about the kitten. They were so excited when they saw it. Stacy said something about your new lady friend having a kitten named Tiger."

Lady friend? Where had Emma gotten that idea? "Oh, you mean the woman who owns the shop? We're just business acquaintances," he explained.

Emma's eyes sparkled. "I see."

Ed accepted the glass of tea and thanked her for taking care of the girls all day. She smiled and said it was her pleasure.

"Okay, girls," he said as he slid into position on the bench across the table from them. "Tell me all about your day."

They both started talking at the same time, which gave him a needed break from his thoughts.

During the Bible study later, Ed focused on the topic of

life's challenges. He paid particular attention when the leader, Jonathan, suggested that during the biggest challenges people needed to learn endurance and dependence on the Lord. "As soon as we think we can control our lives, we've lost the battle."

Ed lowered his head and stared at the floor, thinking about it. Matt's wife sat next to him, and he could see her nudging Matt.

After the Bible study Matt approached him. "Hey, man, you okay?"

"Sure, I'm fine. I just have issues with the topic. I can't seem to get past the whole control thing."

"That's my problem, too." Matt chewed on his lip for a second before adding, "And I suspect Jill might have the same issues."

It always appeared to come back to Jill these days, since she'd been the topic of so many prayers in their group lately. "Yeah, I bet you're right."

"And speaking of Jill, I think it might be a good idea to start moving her on Friday afternoon. We can get some of the big stuff then and at least set her up in the new digs. Then the rest of us can finish up Saturday morning."

Ed nodded. "I'll run it past her."

After he socialized for a few minutes, he left the fellowship hall, fetched his girls, then headed home. They talked nonstop about one of the books their caretaker had read.

"Daddy, did you know Jesus had a brother?" Stacy asked.

"Yes, I did know that."

"But Jesus and His brother weren't twins like us," Tracy said.

Ed didn't have to say another word as the girls discussed how different it would be to have a brother or sister who wasn't a twin. After they got home, they continued their conversation through their bath time and even after he kissed them good night. After he put the girls down, he slipped into bed with his Bible.

The next morning Emma arrived on his doorstep. "I figured you could use a sitter for a few hours this morning. Why don't you run out so you can be back in time for lunch?"

"Are you sure?" he asked. "The girls aren't even up yet."

"Go on—scoot," she said, practically shoving him out the door. "I know you have work to do."

He took advantage of a free morning he hadn't expected and stopped off at the courthouse to find out how the zoning of his new project was coming along. "Looks like the paperwork is almost all done," the clerk said. "It'll only be another couple of weeks, and you're good to go."

"Perfect," Ed said. He left and headed for the shop, where Jill's car was parked by the sidewalk leading to the front door.

When he walked in, she immediately started talking about how Matt and some of the other church people were moving her out early. He'd hoped to be the one to tell her, but she didn't seem upset. In fact, she was more chipper than usual.

"Oh, and Mrs. Cooper called," she said as she grabbed a slip of paper from the desk and handed it to him. "She said her daughter is in the hospital, and she's coming back home until she delivers. She said she'll stop by this evening."

He was relieved to have his sitter back. He knew it was only temporary, but he couldn't worry about that now.

He finished replacing a wall section and reinforced one of the beams, then left to run some more errands before he had to return home. Emma told him she planned to help out with the move.

When Friday arrived, Ed was glad to have Mrs. Cooper there with the girls.

He quickly headed back to the shop where Jill waited on the porch. They walked inside together.

"Ready for the big move?" he asked.

She shrugged and looked around the shop area. "As ready as I'll ever be."

A customer walked in, took a quick look around, and said, "Are you having a going-out-of-business sale already?"

"No," Ed said. "We're just temporarily moving her to a different location so we can fix up this place."

"In that case maybe it'll be good if I do some shopping now. There won't be as much to move."

Ed laughed. Just how much could one woman buy to lighten the load enough to notice?

eight

To his surprise the woman was a professional decorator and made a substantial difference. She purchased quite a bit of glassware and some furniture that she said she'd have out of the shop as soon as her workers could get there later that afternoon.

"Some of these fabulous things will be in the finest homes in Dunwoody," she explained. "Here's my card. Let me know when you get settled. It's certainly nice to have a new source of decorative pieces."

Ed turned to Jill after she left. "A couple of more customers like her, and we won't need people from the church to help move you."

Jill was obviously delighted by her big sale. "At least I'll be able to pay my bills for another month."

The mood instantly lightened. They spent the rest of the day packing. The decorator's people came to pick up her items, and then the remainder of the merchandise was loaded onto trucks.

By mid-Saturday afternoon everything had been moved, and quite a bit had been shelved. The new space turned out to be larger, so nothing had to be put in storage.

On Saturday evening one of the guys called and ordered a dozen pizzas. Ed watched Jill chatting and laughing with the women from the church as if she'd known them all her life. He felt a flutter in his heart when she looked at him with flushed cheeks and a sparkle in her eye. He'd never seen her so happy. And she'd apparently made friends with Jennifer Schwartz, one of the women who'd helped with the move.

Mrs. Cooper had been kind enough to watch the girls all day, so he needed to go home and spend a little time with them before they went to bed. He told Jill he'd see her Monday. She gave him a funny look then nodded. "Are you okay?" he asked.

She nodded, smiling. "I couldn't be better."

❧

On Sunday morning Jill saw the look of utter shock on Ed's face when he spotted her in the church lobby. "Why didn't you tell me you were coming?" he asked.

"Is that a requirement?" she teased. "Do I need to tell you before I go to your church?"

"No, of course not," he said, still obviously flustered. "It's just that—." He took a look around while several people gathered to greet her. "Never mind."

Jennifer tugged on Jill's arm. "C'mon—there's a guy I'd like you to meet."

As Jennifer pulled her away, Jill saw a flash of pain on Ed's face.

It wasn't until Jennifer stopped that Jill turned to her and said, "Well? Where is this guy?"

"Um, let me see," she said as she glanced around. Then her eyes lit up. "There he is!" She pulled Jill toward a cluster of people standing around, talking and laughing. "Jill, meet my dad, the sweetest guy in town. Dad, Mom, this is Jill Hargrove. She's the one who just opened that shop I was telling you about."

It dawned on Jill that Jennifer had intentionally tried to make Ed jealous. She turned to Jennifer's parents and shook their hands. They greeted her with open arms, making Jill feel warm inside. This was how life was supposed to be.

A little while later everyone wandered into the sanctuary to find a seat. Jill sat with Jennifer and her parents. Jennifer's husband, Brian, sang, so he was in the choir loft. She had no idea where Ed was. She did her best to concentrate on what she was there for, but it was difficult knowing Ed was somewhere in the building.

She felt sort of bad because Ed had been inviting her to church practically since they met. And she'd kept turning him down, thinking that one day she'd eventually accept. After he'd left the shop the day before, Jennifer had come up to her and told her what time she was picking her up for church. She hadn't given Jill a choice, so she didn't argue.

This church was completely different than any she'd been to before. These people were truly joyful about their faith.

She thought back to some of her earlier experiences in church with her father. All she could recall were her father's harsh words and the way he had her scared of God's wrath rather than grateful for His love. If it hadn't been for some friends from college who shared the Word with her, she'd still be running from the Lord. She'd pulled out an old Bible and started reading it regularly, using Bible study guides she picked up from Christian bookstores.

During the short time she'd known Ed, he'd shown a different side of faith from her father. He was gentle and kind—like the people from school. Her heart ached as she wondered if her father even knew any better than to present the gospel in such a hurtful way. Ed was obviously a wonderful father to his children and friend to everyone else, including her. She actually had a flicker of a romantic notion toward him, but she quickly squelched it. This wasn't the time to feel romantic toward anyone—not when her business was so new.

A wonderful feeling of peace and contentment rose inside her as she sang the contemporary worship songs. Then they sang a traditional hymn she remembered from childhood. Jennifer nudged her, pointed to the next pew over, and grinned.

Jill glanced over and saw Ed standing there, deeply immersed in his singing. A fresh bolt of attraction shot through her. She'd felt the attraction from the first time she saw him, but this was different. This was a feeling more intense than anything she'd ever experienced. It had more to do with who he was inside than the way he looked.

When she turned back, she saw the odd expression on Jennifer's face. Heat suddenly rose to her cheeks. There was no doubt Jennifer knew exactly what was going on.

The pastor delivered an engaging sermon that kept her spellbound the entire time. Then, when the collection plate came around, she dropped in a visitor envelope with the meager amount she'd stuffed in there. *One of these days I'll be able to give more generously.*

After church Jennifer invited her to join the large group for lunch at a nearby diner. "Who all's going?" Jill asked.

"Everyone in the singles' group," Jennifer replied. "And a few of us married folks who used to be in the singles' group." She gave Jill a nudge. "Come on—Ed'll be there."

"Um, no, thanks. I have some things I need to take care of at home."

Jennifer started to nod then stopped. She gently placed her hand on Jill's shoulder and looked her in the eye. "You should come with us. It's fun."

Again Jill's face heated up. "I know, but. . ."

"Ed's a nice man, and I think he really likes you. I understand you might be feeling a bit overwhelmed by the built-in family, but you couldn't find a nicer guy who loves the Lord more than he does."

Jill was aware of that. Deep down she knew a very large part of her attraction to Ed was his faith. Jennifer was right about her being overwhelmed by the built-in family. As much as she enjoyed Stacy and Tracy, fear of the tremendous responsibility to them was second only to the similarities between Ed and her dad.

"I'm sure," Jill said.

"Look—this is just lunch. We eat lunch and enjoy each other's company. What's the harm in that?"

Jill shrugged.

"If it's any consolation, Ed doesn't usually bring the girls. He's part of a group of parents who take turns with preschoolers so they can each have some fellowship after church."

"Oh, the girls don't bother me," Jill said too quickly. The instant she said it, she saw Jennifer's lips tweak into a smile. To cover, she added, "I've watched them a couple of times, and they're a lot of fun."

"They can be a handful, too."

"I'm sure." Jill clamped her mouth shut to keep from saying the wrong thing.

"So will you go with us?"

Jennifer was quite persuasive and obviously wouldn't let up. Jill nodded. "Yes, but just for a little while."

Brian came up to them, put his arm around his wife, then looked at Jill. "How ya feelin' after the move?" he asked.

Jill grinned. "I'll probably recover about the time I have to move back."

Rather than ride with Brian and Jennifer, Jill chose to follow them to the restaurant, a tiny café that offered a choice of three entrées and a slew of Southern-style vegetables. Country biscuits and corn bread were in baskets on every table. The restaurant had only six tables, but each of them seated eight people. She was relieved when she found an empty chair fairly close to the door. That way she could scoot out when she wanted to leave and hope she wouldn't be noticed.

She managed to avoid Ed until she decided to go home. She'd barely stood up when she saw him approach from the side. There was no way she could take off without appearing rude. She stopped, turned to him, and smiled.

"You have a very nice church," she murmured.

"Thanks." His forehead crinkled, and he looked stressed. "I needed to discuss something with you before I go pick up the girls."

"Um, sure," she said as she glanced around. Several people hastily turned away, so she knew they were watching. "Here?"

"No, let's go outside." He guided her with one hand and opened the door with the other.

As soon as they stepped out into the parking lot he stopped, and she turned toward him. "What's up?" she asked, trying to keep her voice light in spite of the fact that butterflies fluttered from her tummy to her throat.

"Mrs. Cooper warned me that she'd have to pick up and leave on a moment's notice," he said. "I still haven't found anyone to help with the girls."

Jill tilted her head. "So what are you saying?"

He shrugged and looked around, then back at her. "I just wanted you to know in case something happens."

She nodded. "Okay, I understand."

Ed looked at her with an odd expression; then he side-stepped away from her. "Well, I guess I need to go back and tell everyone bye. See ya tomorrow?"

"See you then," Jill replied as she headed for her car.

❧

Ed felt like the idiot of the year for making such a big deal out of nothing. They'd already discussed Mrs. Cooper's daughter, and Jill was well aware of what was happening. She didn't seem to have a problem with him bringing his daughters to her shop, so she certainly wouldn't say anything about them now that she was in his warehouse. They'd known each other long enough for him to realize she was a decent woman with a heart. A big heart, in fact. The way she'd softened had puzzled him at first, but when he got over the surprise, he'd let down his guard and allowed himself to be swayed by her sweetness. Yes, he'd known her long enough to see many sides of her, and with the exception of her initial skittishness he liked what he saw.

And he'd known her long enough to start feeling the pangs he thought he'd never have again. They were odd sensations, those pangs. When he looked at Jill, tenderness overcame him, and he felt immensely protective. When she looked at him or when they talked, he cared about what she thought. And when they touched—whether on purpose or accidentally—an electrical sensation shot all the way through him, straight to his heart. Her vulnerability added to his attraction.

If Jill hadn't been a Christian, he could have found the strength to continue avoiding social situations with her. She'd told him she was a believer and that she read the Bible, but he hadn't been certain she was all that committed to her faith. When he saw her in church, though, he noticed the sincerity in her eyes and how she was completely wrapped up in what the pastor was saying. He wasn't 100 percent sure, but at least it gave him some hope that her faith was real.

Then he did a mental slap to the forehead. Hope for what? A deeper-than-friends relationship? She'd made it perfectly clear she didn't want any more responsibility than she already had. And his girls needed constant attention.

He'd just have to settle for being Jill's friend. But that thought didn't appeal to him.

The girls were all giggles when he picked them up. Apparently one of the puppet ministry leaders had done an impromptu show for the kids, and they loved it. They were exhausted, too, but since it was a little past nap time Ed decided to keep them up until after dinner so they'd go to bed early.

His plan worked, except here he was at seven thirty on a

Sunday night, virtually alone. He had way too much time to think, so he flipped on the TV. Nothing there but mindless sitcoms and talking-head news shows. He found his Bible and started looking for something to calm him and keep his mind off Jill.

No matter what verse he turned to, something about Jill popped into his head. It seemed she'd taken over all his waking and most of his sleeping thoughts. The woman was tiny in person, but she loomed very large when she wasn't present.

Finally, after giving in and accepting what was happening, Ed sat back and read the book of James. As long as he focused on the Word, he could find peace in almost any situation.

He had the first restful night in weeks. When he awoke to two energetic little girls jumping on his bed, he propped up on his elbows and grinned at them. "Whatcha want for breakfast?" He knew it would likely be something dripping in sticky, sweet syrup or something from a fast-food place.

"Waffles!" they both shouted.

"Then waffles it is," he said as he sat up and slowly swung his legs to the side. "Go get dressed, and I'll meet you in the kitchen in about fifteen minutes."

Stacy arrived in the kitchen wearing her shorts backward. He smiled. Tracy had her shirt buttoned in the wrong holes, making the hem lopsided. He wouldn't trade precious moments like these for anything.

The day started off great, and Ed felt as if nothing could go wrong. Mrs. Cooper arrived humming a hymn, and the girls both gave her a great big hug. Everyone was happy, the sun was shining, and Ed was raring to go. Since Jill's shop was being fumigated and he couldn't do anything there, he'd decided to use this time to run errands and finish some of the legwork for his new development. He was close to breaking ground.

But first he stopped off at the warehouse to make sure Jill

was okay. She pulled into the parking lot at the same time. He took a long look at her to gauge her mood, and to his delight she was smiling.

"You were a hit with everyone at church yesterday," Ed said.

"So it's a popularity contest?" she teased.

"You know what I mean." He could tell by her smile and how her voice lilted that she was just being playful and not sarcastic.

"I'm glad I finally went," she admitted. "It's nothing like how I remember church being. Things have really changed."

Ed wondered if the only thing that had changed was her attitude, but he didn't want to dampen her spirit or insult her. So he brought up a new subject.

"So—ready to get started in the new digs?" he asked.

She offered a quick nod as she walked comfortably around the makeshift shop, turning on lights and moving a few things around. "To be honest, I thought it would take several days to get everything the way I wanted it, but it's almost as if I've been here forever."

"That's what happens when you have more than a dozen people working on it."

"Are the people in your church always this helpful?" she asked as she slipped behind the counter.

"Most of the time," he replied. "We have a nice group of believers. They take their commitment to their faith very seriously."

"Yes, I can certainly see that."

Ed studied her until he heard the bell he'd hung over the door jingling. A customer. He turned around and saw a whole group of people from the church.

"Hey, we wanted to be the first to shop in your new location," Jennifer said as she led the pack inside. "We all saw something we wanted to buy, so here we are."

Ed hung around for a few minutes until he realized he wasn't needed. Then he told Jill he had some things to do. She told him she could handle the crowd, and he agreed.

Thank You, Lord, he mouthed as he slid into his truck.

❧

Jill sensed a change in Ed. He was as sure of himself as ever, but she caught him watching her as if he wasn't sure about her.

Being honest with herself, she knew she'd undergone some monumental changes since meeting Ed. She'd learned to accept help from someone else without feeling as if she had to offer payment for every little thing. And she realized that staying away from church simply because of her own bad experience as a child was just plain ridiculous. She should have known better than to judge anyone else based on something that had happened with her father.

Jill had brought her Bible to work with her. Between waiting on customers, she read over the scripture verses the pastor had referred to in his sermon. She loved hearing him talk. He had a wonderful way of relating everything biblical to current Christian living. This was something she'd missed when she'd isolated herself from other believers.

Another customer came in, so Jill slid the Bible beneath the counter. She answered a bunch of questions; then the bell sounded at the door again. When she glanced up she was surprised to see Ed's girls trailing behind their nanny.

She grinned. "Mrs. Cooper." Jill took a step toward the woman, her hand extended, but she pulled back when it became evident the woman was frazzled.

"I have an emergency, and Ed's not answering his cell phone," the woman said. "My daughter's in labor, and she's having some complications." She gestured toward the girls. "I'm not sure—"

Jill held up her hand. "Don't worry about a thing, Mrs. Cooper. Leave the girls with me, and go do what you need to do." She looked down at the twins. "We'll be fine, won't we, girls?"

Stacy and Tracy looked at each other, then back at her, nodding. "We like Jill," Tracy said softly.

"We *love* Jill," Stacy added.

Jill felt a fullness in her chest as an emotion she'd never experienced before welled inside her.

"If you're sure. . ." Mrs. Cooper had already let go of the girls' hands and taken a step toward the door. Jill could see how worried the woman was.

"I'm positive," Jill assured her. "Now go be with your daughter. Call Ed later and let him know how everything is." She waited until Mrs. Cooper had her hand on the door. "I'll let others at the church know we need to pray for you and your daughter."

After Mrs. Cooper left, Stacy jumped up and down, clapping her hands. "Can we be salesladies?" she asked.

Jill chuckled. "I doubt that's legal with child labor laws."

"Child what?" Stacy asked, her forehead scrunched in confusion.

"Never mind." Jill gently guided the girls to the area behind her desk. "Let's get the two of you set up back here. I think I might have some art supplies. You do like to make things, don't you?"

Both girls nodded enthusiastically, so Jill grabbed a bunch of crayons and the pack of colored computer paper she'd purchased to make signs and plopped them down at a child-sized table. She pulled up a little chair and an old milk crate. "I only have one regular chair," she apologized.

"I want that one," Stacy said, pointing to the milk crate.

Tracy pouted. "It's my turn to pick."

"Wait," Jill said, holding up her hands. "If you both want to sit on milk crates, I have more. Just give me a few seconds."

She quickly had them set up with something to do for a little while—or at least until she could think of something else. She hoped Ed wouldn't be gone long.

Unfortunately, whatever business he had took longer than the children's attention span, so Jill had to think of something else. She was going through a mental list of what she used to enjoy at that age when Stacy had a brilliant idea.

"Let's have a tea party!" she said. "You have some children's teacups over there." She pointed to the demitasse set Jill had just brought in.

Jill paused. She was pretty sure they were valuable. But what did it matter? They weren't terribly expensive, and she could wash them and sell them later. Besides, the set included twelve. If one of them broke, she'd just have one less cup to sell. No big deal.

"Fine," Jill said. "But I don't have anything to put in them."

Tracy tapped her chin with her tiny finger. Jill's heart warmed as she watched the child ponder. Suddenly Tracy's face lit up. "Daddy sometimes lets us have ginger ale for tea parties."

Stacy placed her hands on her hips, and in her bossy manner blurted out, "And where we gonna get ginger ale, Miss Smarty Pants?"

It took everything Jill had not to crack up laughing. The bell over the door jingled again. Jill glanced up, hoping Ed had come to her rescue. But it wasn't Ed. It was Jennifer from church.

"Hey, how's my favorite antique shop doing?"

Jill had an idea. "If I give you a couple of dollars, would you mind running over to that convenience store across the street and picking up a bottle of ginger ale?"

"Be glad to," Jennifer said as she ran out the door before Jill had a chance to give her the money.

While Jennifer was gone, Jill found two more milk crates

for herself and Jennifer. If they were having a tea party, they might as well do it right. She carried the demitasse cups and saucers to the big sink Ed had in his workshop area, scrubbed the cups, then dried them with paper towels. Before Jennifer returned, she had four places set up at the tiny table.

Stacy and Tracy found a couple of dolls and asked if they could have tea with them. Jill didn't hesitate to say that was fine, in spite of the fact that one of the dolls was worth hundreds of dollars.

"Just be careful," Jill warned. "She's fragile."

"What's 'fragile'?" Stacy asked.

"It means you have to be very gentle with her. She breaks easily."

Stacy nodded her understanding. "We'll be very careful."

"Is my doll fragile?" Tracy asked, holding up the one she'd selected.

"Yes," Jill replied. Tracy's doll wasn't as valuable on the market, but to Tracy she probably was. "Y'all want to invite Jennifer to join us?"

Both girls immediately nodded.

Jill was glad when Jennifer finally returned, holding up a bag with ginger ale. "I got some cookies for the girls. I hope that's okay."

Jennifer's eyes lit up when Stacy told her she was invited to a real live tea party. "Ooh, it's been a long time since I've done this. Thanks! Where should I sit?"

The four of them were seated on milk crates, sipping ginger ale from demitasse cups, and telling silly animal jokes when Jill heard someone clearing his throat by the door. She quickly spun around to see Ed propped against the door, his arms folded, and one leg draped over the other, a grin playing on his lips.

Jill hopped up. "Did you need something?" She glanced over her shoulder at the tea party, then back at him. "Oh, Mrs.

Cooper's daughter is in labor, so I agreed to watch the twins. Would you like some ginger ale?"

"Don't let me interrupt," he replied as he pulled away from his position. He ambled a few feet toward his office area. "When you're finished, send the girls back here."

nine

Seeing his daughters having the time of their lives with Jill and Jennifer caused a swell of emotion in Ed's chest. He'd known Jennifer for years, but until now she'd never made an effort with his daughters. She always said she wasn't "into kids." Well, Jill had said essentially the same thing, and now look at them.

"Daddy, look!" Stacy said. He stopped and turned around to face her. "We have fragile dolls."

Tracy nodded. "Yeah, we have to be very careful not to break them."

Ed lifted one eyebrow and looked over toward Jill, who forced a straight face. Jennifer kept darting her glance back and forth between him and Jill.

"Would you like something to drink?" Jill repeated.

"We're having ginger ale tea, Daddy," Stacy explained.

Ed felt as if he'd walked in on a private party he hadn't been invited to, and he wasn't sure what to do. "Uh, no. I think I'll go back to my office and get some work done. Jill, when you're finished with your, uh, party, can we talk?"

Jennifer chose that moment to speak up. "If you two need to talk, I can watch the sales floor for a few minutes."

"No—," Jill said at the same time Ed spoke. "That would be great."

Jennifer cleared her throat. "Just let me know, okay?"

Ed headed to his office, but he propped the door open so he could keep an eye on his daughters. The ginger ale tea party lasted another five minutes until the girls suddenly lost interest. He jumped up and grabbed Stacy as she darted past shelves of cookware and toward some ceramic figurines.

"Okay, squirt, why don't you and your sister work on some puzzles I picked up while I was out?"

"Puzzles?" Stacy said, looking around.

"Back here." He led them to the makeshift table he'd set up a long time ago for days when he had them.

Tracy walked up to Jill and tugged on her hand. "Is it okay with you if we play with puzzles?"

"Of course it's okay. Why wouldn't it be?"

With her hands out to her sides Tracy shrugged. "I don't want you to think we don't want to play with you anymore. We like you a lot."

Ed watched as tears instantly formed in Jill's eyes. She sniffled and turned slightly so he couldn't see her expression. "I like you a lot, too, sweetie. But I have to go back to work, so it's just fine if you want to play with puzzles."

Warmth flooded Ed. He could feel himself falling for Jill, but the relationship between his daughters and Jill had caught him off guard. What shocked him the most, though, was how it affected him. He was torn between joy over Stacy and Tracy finding a female adult to look up to and concern that Jill would break their hearts. Breaking *his* heart would be bad enough, but he could handle it.

"C'mon, girls. Let's let Jill do her work. You've taken up enough of her time."

"Wait a minute," Jill said in a tone of authority he'd never heard from her before. "They haven't taken up my time. I had a tea party with them because I wanted to and not for any other reason."

"I didn't mean—"

"Contrary to what you might believe, Ed Mathis, I like your daughters. I might not have much experience with kids, but I'll play tea party with Stacy and Tracy anytime they want me to."

"Okay," he said softly, holding up his hands and taking another step away. "Sorry. I didn't mean anything by it."

Jill backed toward her showroom. He went into his office after he heard her chatting with Jennifer.

The girls were now busy with their puzzles, and Jill was safely in her space up front. This was the perfect time to do paperwork on his new development. The problem now was that he couldn't concentrate. All he could think about was Jill and how she made him feel. Her warmth and kindness when she let down her guard. Her generosity with her customers and his daughters. . .and with him when he least expected it. He felt as if he were being pulled toward her by some irresistible force he couldn't control. He kept hoping that would fade, but with each passing day she took up more and more of his waking thoughts.

His awareness of Jill's every move rendered him incapable of doing his own work. He finally gave up and started doing some physical labor. He liked to saw and hammer when he needed a physical release of any pent-up emotions.

"Daddy, are you mad at us?" Stacy asked from the table.

He stopped sawing the piece of wood and turned to face the girls. "No, of course not. Why do you think I'm mad?"

Stacy looked at Tracy, who shrugged. "Your face is red, like when you get mad at us for jumping on the bed."

Ed let out a breath and put down his saw. He crossed over to the girls and squatted beside them. "Girls, I'm not mad at anyone. It's just that I'm thinking about things you wouldn't understand."

"Are you thinking about Jill?" Tracy asked.

He started to deny that he was, but the girls could see right through him. He nodded. "Sometimes, yes."

The twins faced each other and exchanged knowing smiles. "We thought so."

"Jill needs a lot of help from us, and I'm trying to figure out what to do next."

"We can help, Daddy. We love Jill."

"Thanks, kiddos. Now get back to your puzzles, and I'll see if there's anything Jill needs before we go home."

⁂

When Ed appeared by the cash register, Jill jumped. "Sorry if I scared you," he said. "I just wanted to see if there was anything I could do for you before I take the girls home."

She slowly shook her head. "No, I'm fine, but thanks."

He moved toward the door. "C'mon, girls—let's get a move on." The girls dropped what they were doing and ran to his side. "See ya tomorrow, Jill." He nodded toward Jennifer. "G'night, Jen."

Both girls ran up to Jill, wrapped their arms around her waist, and gave her a squeeze. A lump of emotion filled her chest as she reached down and patted them on the back. Then just as quickly as they'd come to her, they went back to their dad, waved bye, and were out the door. *Stacy and Tracy are little whirlwinds,* she thought as she retreated to a small space behind some shelves where she could pretend to arrange stock while recovering from her emotions.

As difficult as it was for Jill to admit, even to herself, her business had taken off like a lightning bolt shortly after Ed came into her life. In fact, it was better than anything she'd ever expected. Her regular customers—many of them elderly women who bought out of nostalgia—were taken in by Ed's charm. And the people from the church were extremely supportive—even people who'd never collected antiques.

To top things off, Ed's church seemed like the kind of place she'd want to plug into for worship and friendship. But the very fact he was there all the time put a kink in that. With the attraction she felt toward him, she knew she was treading on dangerous ground. If he'd been footloose without children and she didn't have a brand-new business, she might not have felt so overwhelmed by the man. His having a built-in family gave her pause. Sure, she loved the girls, but they were a handful. She could tell they needed more than she'd ever be able to give.

"Hey, Jill, want to go out with some folks from the church? We're grabbing a burger and seeing a movie tonight." Jennifer had found her and was standing at the edge of the shelves, holding an old book filled with pictures of collectibles.

"I'm afraid not tonight," Jill replied.

"Let me buy this book; then I gotta run."

Jill fluttered her hand. "You don't have to buy it. Just borrow it and bring it back when you're finished."

Jennifer looked as if she was about to argue, but she clamped her mouth shut and nodded. "That'll be great. I won't keep it long."

"Keep it as long as you need it. I have another copy on the shelves."

Jill was glad to be alone. It had been awhile since she'd had time to gather her thoughts; the move and the church had taken her by storm.

That afternoon when Jill tallied receipts, she was surprised at how well the shop had done—and at the same time how much she'd enjoyed the day. She'd always heard about the joy of having a career she could love, and now she was seeing it truly could happen. She felt a peace she'd never had before.

Later that week, the exterminator called to say he couldn't get started because of a cat that kept darting under the tent. She'd searched for Tiger before she left, but when she couldn't find her she figured the kitten had found another home. When Jill told Ed about Tiger, he jumped into action. He and Matt went over there, and Ed finally managed to coax a very scared and hungry Tiger into his truck. Jill's heart melted at the sight of muscular Ed holding the adolescent kitten who'd grown dependent on her.

Jill found a small plastic bowl and filled it with some of the cat food Ed had remembered to pick up on his way to rescue Tiger. The kitten seemed very grateful as she settled down for a hearty meal while Ed and Jill stood back and watched. That night Jill took Tiger home with her.

"The cat set us back on timing. Looks like it'll be another couple of weeks before they can start the extermination," Ed told her the next morning. "They're having to work your job in between some that were already scheduled. And then I still need to repair the floor and walls."

As eager as Jill was to be back in her own space, she took a deep breath, slowly let it out, and said, "That's fine, as long as you don't mind me being here."

Ed stood still and looked at her, tenderness in his eyes, his jaw relaxed. Jill wanted to reach out and trace the side of his face, but she held back, hoping the urge would pass. It didn't.

"Jill," he said softly, "you may stay in the warehouse as long as it takes to—"

At that moment the bell sounded on the door, interrupting him. Jill turned around and glanced out the glass door. She noticed a large tour bus parked outside. A couple of women stood at the counter, chattering up a storm.

"May I help you?" Jill asked.

"Yes," one of the women said. "We saw the sign on the Junktique Shoppe lawn about being in a temporary location. Is this the right place?"

Confused, Jill nodded. "Yes, this is the place."

"Oh, good," the other woman said. "Let's go tell everyone."

As the two women headed out to the bus, Jill looked at Ed quizzically. He grinned. "Oh, I forgot to tell you; I had a big sign made for the yard. I didn't want you to lose any business."

Within a couple of minutes, the shop was teeming with about thirty middle-aged and elderly women, all of them loading up on knickknacks and other glassware. One woman had a basket she was filling with linens. Jill stood at the cash register, astonished at the booming business. She also knew she'd have to hustle and get more merchandise, or she'd be out of business due to not having anything to sell.

After the group left a couple of hours later, Jill stood in the center of the store and took a long look around. Ed had helped out, and he was putting a few discarded items back on the shelves.

"I have no idea what just happened," Jill said. "But it's obvious I can't keep up with it by myself."

Ed chuckled. "I bet you can probably find a few people from the church who'd love to work part-time while you go on a buying spree to replace some of this stuff."

"I'll have to look into it," she agreed.

"Better make it soon." He started back to his work area when he suddenly stopped, pivoted around to face her, and said, "Oh, by the way, the girls wanted to know if we could pick you up for church on Sunday."

She'd gone to church alone the past couple of Sundays, but the minute she stepped out of her car she'd found herself surrounded by her new friends. That was wonderful, except that Ed always seemed to be on the outside looking in. He could have made his way to her, but she noticed his hesitation. Until now.

"Tell the girls that would be nice."

Ed blinked, almost as if he wasn't sure he'd heard right. "Eight thirty okay? We can stop off and have breakfast somewhere on the way."

Jill nodded slowly. "I'd like that."

On Sunday morning Jill opened her door and was greeted by the twins, who stood there alone. "Where's your daddy?" she asked.

Stacy pointed behind them. "He's in the truck waiting. We told him we were big enough to come and get you by ourselves."

Tracy nodded. "He had to unbuckle Stacy's car seat, but I got mine undone all by myself." She tilted her head. "I'm getting big cuz I'll be five next week."

Jill had to stifle a smile as she took a step back. "Come on in while I get a sweater."

The girls giggled as they stepped into her cottage. "Do you live here all by yourself?" Tracy asked.

"Yes, I sure do," Jill replied.

"Aren't you scared?"

"No, not really."

Stacy nodded. "I know why. Jesus is always with you."

Jill beamed down at Stacy. "Yes, you're absolutely right. As long as He's by my side, I don't have to be afraid of anything."

Tracy looked down at her feet, then back up at Jill, her lips turned downward in a frown. "Sometimes I still get afraid."

Jill leaned down and cupped Tracy's face in her hands. "Honestly, I think everyone gets afraid at times. But that's normal."

"What do you get afraid of?" Stacy asked.

Being alone for the rest of my life, she thought, although there was no way she'd say that to a couple of almost-five-year-olds. "I dunno. Just silly things, like if people will keep coming to my store."

"We'll come to your store anytime you want us to," Stacy said with confidence.

Jill had to fight back tears of joy that they seemed so happy to be part of her life. "Come to my store anytime."

The three of them left the cottage and headed for Ed's truck, where he sat smiling. "Want me to sit in the back?" she asked as she opened the door. "We can put one of the girls up here with you."

Both girls shook their heads. "No!"

Ed patted the passenger seat. "I promise I won't bite."

Stacy started giggling; then Tracy chimed in. Snorting, Stacy said, "My daddy wouldn't even bite a dog if it bit him first." That made both of them laugh.

Ed glanced at his girls in the rearview mirror, then turned to wink at Jill. "They've heard me say that," he whispered. He looked back at the girls. "I wouldn't be too sure about that."

That sent the girls into another fit of giggles. The happiness level in the cab of Ed's truck was higher than Jill had experienced during her entire childhood. And she loved the way it felt to be a part of it. Ed gave her a sense of well-being and belonging. The girls were a wonderful bonus.

Ed pulled his truck into a tiny diner that specialized in breakfast and lunch. Jill had seen it before, but she'd never eaten there.

"Tracy and I like fast-food pancakes," Stacy said.

"But Daddy said you'd like this place, so we told him that was okay," Tracy added. "We want you to have fun with us."

Jill's heart melted a little bit more. "Thanks, but if you'd rather go for fast food, that's fine."

Ed turned off the ignition and cast a silly look at his girls before turning back to her. "I told them not to tell you that," he said.

"But, Daddy, we wanted her to know we're doing this special for her."

Jill unbuckled her seat belt and climbed out before helping them out of their seats in the back. Tracy had hers undone and was busy working on Stacy's until Jill took over. "I'm happy to have such nice friends who like to do special things for me."

Once Stacy was on the ground, she looked up at Jill and, with an expression that looked more grown-up than ever, said, "You did something special for us when we had that tea party."

"I loved that tea party," Jill said quickly.

"We know that," Stacy said with confidence as she took Jill's hand. "We all liked it. Even Jennifer."

"Especially Jennifer," Jill said.

Ed cupped his hands over his mouth and whispered, "Remind me to tell you something after we drop off the girls at their classroom."

"Are you gonna tell her Jennifer used to be scared of children before?" Stacy asked.

A goofy look came over Ed's face, and Jill laughed. Ed obviously couldn't pull anything over on his girls; they were so smart.

"Jennifer is a very nice lady," Ed said. "Let's change the subject, okay?"

After breakfast they drove to the church. The parking lot was almost full. "I'll take the girls to their classroom," Ed said. "Why don't you go find a good seat?"

"Don't sit in the back," Stacy said. "Daddy hates sitting in the back."

The back was Jill's favorite place to sit in church, but after what Stacy said she didn't stop there. She found a nice spot toward the front and on the very edge of the pew. Ed joined her a few minutes later.

"What did you want to tell me that you couldn't say in front of the girls?" Jill asked.

"Stacy pretty much covered it," he whispered. "I think you might have changed things."

The choir started singing, so Jill didn't have a chance to respond. She focused on the overhead screen and sang the worship songs until it was time for the sermon. Ed's presence next to her was somewhat distracting, but she still enjoyed the message.

After church Ed stood and faced her. "Well, would you like to go to lunch?"

Jill pursed her lips. She would have loved to go to lunch, but she didn't want to overdo things with Ed.

She shook her head. "I don't think so. Not today."

"You sure?" he asked as he folded his arms and frowned.

"Positive," she replied before she had a chance to change her mind. "I have a ton of stuff to do at home. You know how things can pile up when you work all week."

"Yes," he said as he sighed. "I do know."

Jill sat and waited for him as he ran around to the other side and got in. "Where are the girls?"

"They're with some friends."

Once they were on their way, Jill started chattering about how much she enjoyed Stacy and Tracy. "They're obviously well-adjusted and super smart. I've enjoyed them quite a bit."

Ed grinned. "Thanks. I think so, too, but I figured that was just the proud father in me coming out." He paused before adding, "The girls really like you, too."

The warmth in his voice touched Jill.

When he pulled up, Jill started to jump out of the truck. But Ed reached over and gently placed his hand on her shoulder. "Jill," he said, "can we talk?"

ten

She turned to face him. "What did you want to talk about?"

He ran his thumb along the edge of the steering wheel as he sat in silence for several very long, uncomfortable seconds. Finally, when he spoke, his voice cracked. "Jill, I really like you."

"I like you, too, Ed."

"My girls are crazy about you."

Now it was Jill's turn to pause. "I, uh, well. . .I like them a lot."

The expression on Ed's face remained unreadable. She could tell his guard was up.

"You're different from what I thought when I first met you."

Jill tilted her head and looked at him. "What do you mean?"

He shrugged. "You're very responsible."

She couldn't help but laugh. "You didn't think I was responsible at first? You thought I was a flake." That last comment had slipped out, and she regretted saying it the instant she saw the mortified look on his face.

"I never said you were a flake."

Jill reached out and placed her hand on his arm. "I know. I was just kidding. Is this what you wanted to talk about?"

"I just wanted you to understand why we have to be careful. When Marcy found out she had gestational diabetes, we assumed it was simply a complication that would disappear as soon as the twins were born. We had no idea it would be. . . fatal."

Jill's heart ached at the very thought of what Ed and the girls had been through. "I'm so sorry."

"I can't take a chance on letting the girls get hurt by someone who might break their hearts, as unintentional as it would be."

"That's understandable, but I don't plan to break their hearts. I can be their friend, can't I?"

"Their friend?"

Jill nodded. "That's what I am. Their friend." She glanced down, then decided to take a chance on letting her feelings out a little more. "Actually, I adore the girls more than I can explain. I never realized how children could make such a difference in my outlook on life."

He smiled at her tenderly. "You've made a huge difference in *our* outlook on life."

She blinked. He'd included himself. "Ed, you're a very special man."

A sheepish look came across his face, and then he turned to face her. "I'm just doing what any man would do in my shoes."

Jill swallowed hard. Ed's goodness ran so deep that he didn't realize he'd done much more than what most men would have done. He'd taken on the role of being the father and the mother to his little girls. He'd taken them to church without showing any signs of bitterness toward God. And he'd reached out to her, taken her under his wing, and made sure she didn't lose her business.

"Ready to go in?" he asked as he reached for the handle. She nodded. "Oh, one more thing. I'm having a birthday party for the girls next weekend. Can you come?"

She nodded. "Yes, of course."

He helped her out of the truck and took her by the hand. Jill felt a natural, warm glow as they walked up the sidewalk to her house.

When they reached the door, she turned to face him. She had the odd sensation they were supposed to kiss. But they didn't. Instead he stood there looking at her for several seconds before he let go of her hand, turned, said, "See ya tomorrow," then left.

When Jill was inside, she closed the door, leaned against it, and shut her eyes. She was so not prepared for this. All she'd ever wanted was to lead a quiet life alone with her own little shop to run, no one telling her what to do and not having to account for a thing. And here she was, attending a lively, energetic church and falling in love with a man with two kids. How could she deal with it? With a sigh she closed her eyes and swallowed hard before she prayed.

Lord, I've loved You for a long time, and that's all I really need. I'm sure You had the best of intentions when You brought Ed into my life, but he's not what I need right now.

Then suddenly her eyes popped open. An alarm sounded in her head. The sermon that very morning had been about trying to tell God what to do. Pastor Travers had said people needed to be still and listen. God knew what they needed without their having to say a single word.

Jill frantically moved about her house, straightening pillows on the couch, picking up tufts of cat hair from the carpet, and, when she reached the kitchen, loading her dishwasher. Then she filled the dispenser with detergent, shut the door, and hit the power button. From there she headed to her room, where she put away yesterday's clothes and made the bed.

Once she was finished she sucked in a deep breath and took a long look around. She'd just done housework. That was totally not like her. To top it off, she felt good about it. What was going on?

She spent the rest of the afternoon doing laundry and studying magazines about collectibles. Then she thought about what to get the girls for their birthday.

Throughout the next week Ed acted distant, although he

was pleasant. He'd found someone to watch the girls during the day, so she didn't see them. To her surprise and dismay, she missed them. Whenever she heard a child's voice or laughter, her heart thudded until she realized it was only a customer's child and not Stacy or Tracy.

On Saturday she'd just finished helping a customer load an old wooden desk into the back of her SUV when Ed pulled into the parking lot with his daughters. She instinctively smiled when they bounded out of the truck, grins on their precious little faces, arms open wide, coming toward her at full speed. She squatted down and pulled them in for a hug as Ed stood behind them, watching.

"The girls wanted to pick you up for their birthday party," he said.

"Thank you." Jill stood, looked at each girl, and gestured toward her shop. "Come on in, girls. I have something for you."

They followed her inside to the little table in the back where Jill had put a stack of wrapped educational toys and games she'd picked up last time she went to the store. It took them about a minute to tear open the wrapping paper. "You got all that stuff for us?" Stacy asked.

Jill nodded. "Who else would I get it for? You're my favorite little birthday girls."

Tracy turned to Ed. "Daddy, is it okay if we play here for a little while?"

Ed twisted his mouth in the comical way Jill loved, glanced at his watch, then nodded. "Well, I s'pose it'll be okay. The party isn't for another couple of hours."

Jill started to go back to her sales floor when she heard Tracy call out. "Can you go to church with us again?"

Stopping in her tracks, Jill tried to make a quick decision. She couldn't think of a single reason to say no—at least, not one the children would understand. And since it was one of the girls asking, she simply nodded and said, "Sure, if it's okay with your daddy."

"It's okay with Daddy," Stacy said.

Jill glanced over her shoulder at Ed. He held her gaze for a couple of seconds then nodded. "We'll be out of town tomorrow, but I'd like for you to go with us next week."

"Okay," she said.

An hour before the party was due to start, they headed to Ed's house so he could finish setting up. Jill helped the girls slip into their party dresses. Children from the neighborhood and church came by with their parents. The party lasted an hour, but it seemed much shorter to Jill. Once the last guest left, though, both girls went to their room and fell asleep right away. Ed asked his neighbor, Mrs. McKnight, to come in and watch the girls while he took Jill back to the shop where she'd left her car.

"I had a wonderful time, Ed," Jill said.

Ed took her hands in his and pulled her closer. "Thank you for everything," he whispered. She started to pull away, but he wouldn't let go. Instead he leaned over and gave her a light kiss on the lips. Then he walked her to her car.

She had plans to go to church with Jennifer the next day. Ed had taken the girls to their grandmother's house to celebrate their birthday because she hadn't been able to attend the party.

The next week dragged by. As much as Jill loved her shop and handling the collectibles, she found herself wanting to spend more and more time with Ed and the girls. But now that he had broken ground on his property development in Ackworth, she saw little of him.

The next Sunday finally arrived. As before, Ed waited in the truck while Stacy and Tracy went to Jill's door. Only this time she'd expected them.

"Here's a surprise," she said as she handed each of them a tiny stuffed animal.

Their eyes lit up. "You got these just for us?"

Jill nodded. "Absolutely, yes."

Tracy cuddled hers close to her chest with one hand and reached for Jill's hand with the other while Stacy ran ahead of them, her arm outstretched with the stuffed kitten. "Looky, Daddy! Looky what Jill got me!"

Ed gave her a puzzled look. "You don't have to give them presents every time you see them."

"I know," she said. "It's just that I know they like kittens, and I saw these in the store, and—"

"You couldn't resist," Ed said, finishing her sentence. "Yeah, I know how that goes. Happens to me all the time."

Ed hopped out to help settle the girls in the backseat, then slid back behind the wheel.

"If you want me to quit buying them stuff, I will," Jill said softly as she got in and buckled her seat belt.

"Once in a while is nice," Ed said. "But they just had a birthday, and I think the real prize is getting to see you."

As silence fell over them, Jill pondered his last comment, which she found immensely flattering. But was he talking about the real prize for the girls or for him? She knew the girls enjoyed having her around. They'd made that obvious. But how about Ed? Did he look forward to seeing her as much as she did him?

"Whatcha thinkin'?" he asked as they turned down the street leading to the church.

She shrugged. "That I'm grateful for your church and all the nice people who go there."

෴

Ed pulled into the parking lot, found a spot, then turned to look at her. She continued to soften each time he saw her.

When he'd first walked into her shop she was defensive, and he suspected she could have been combative if tested. But now he'd seen her soft side, and it was incredibly appealing. Almost everything about Jill was appealing—even her tendency to be messy, which had bugged him to no end when he first met her.

The sense of belonging washed over him as he stood next to Jill during the worship part of the service. When the pastor spoke, Ed slanted occasional glances her way and saw the intensity of her interest. Warmth flooded him as he thought about how absorbed in the Word she seemed.

After church, as soon as they fetched the girls from their Sunday school class, Stacy said, "Daddy, can we get a kids' meal?"

"I don't see why not," he replied. He turned to Jill. "Unless, of course, you have to be home at any particular time."

She shrugged. "I really don't have anything else to do today, so that sounds good. I haven't had fast food in quite a while."

"Good. Then let's go."

Jill chatted with the girls while he returned to his deep-thought mode. The cozy feeling he had was wonderful until he actually gave it some serious thought. He, Jill, and the girls seemed like family. The problem was—they weren't. Was he setting the girls up for disappointment when Jill got tired of them?

Ed ordered their kids' meals and handed them to the girls.

"Eat first," he said. "Then you can play." He turned to Jill. "Is it okay with you if we sit in the kiddy area? That way we won't have to move when they're on the equipment."

"Sure," she said, taking her tray and heading to the small dining tables in the back.

Stacy and Tracy scarfed down their food in warp speed. They were finished and had their spots on the table cleaned before Jill had time to eat half her sandwich.

Laughing, Jill said, "Now I know what to do if I want a kid to eat."

Ed nodded. "It works."

❧

Jill felt as though she belonged. She was more relaxed than she could ever remember being.

They spent the next hour watching the girls, chatting about church, and basically keeping the conversation light. Once in a while the girls came over to make sure Ed had seen something they'd done.

"How about some ice cream?" Ed asked.

Both girls nodded and hopped up and down. Ed took the girls to the counter and purchased a small ice cream cone for each of them; then he sat back down with Jill while the girls enjoyed their dessert before going back to play on the equipment.

About a half hour later Stacy came over to them. "Daddy, I want a cookie."

"No, honey, you've already had your dessert."

She glared at him, folded her arms, and stamped her foot. "I want a cookie."

Tracy was right behind her. "Please, Daddy, please. Can't we have a cookie?"

"No," Ed said firmly. "One dessert is plenty. You don't need that much sugar."

Then to Jill's dismay both girls started screaming and throwing a temper tantrum. She'd never seen this side of them and shrank back in her seat.

Ed tried to talk calmly to the girls, but it was obvious he wasn't getting anywhere. Finally he took both girls by the hand and held on tight. "This temper tantrum is not acceptable behavior," he said firmly. "So we're going home now."

"No!" Tracy shouted. "I wanna play some more."

Stacy managed to break free of Ed's grasp. She took off

running toward the play area.

Ed turned to Jill and offered an apologetic grin. "Sorry about this. Would you mind taking over with Tracy while I go get Stacy?"

Jill gulped hard as Ed took Tracy's hand and placed it in Jill's. That terrible feeling from her own childhood hit her full force. Her father had rules that were so rigid she'd felt stifled. And here she was, participating in discipline. But she understood it now.

Tracy kept scowling while Jill held tight to her hand. What bugged Jill was that Tracy wasn't even looking at her. In fact, Jill was pretty sure Tracy hated her for being on Ed's side, and that broke her heart. If it had been up to her, she probably would have given them the cookie. What did it matter, anyway? They hadn't eaten that much ice cream. But then again she saw Ed's side, too. The instant the tantrum started, it was a matter of principle. She realized Ed couldn't let them have the upper hand when they behaved like this.

Eventually Stacy got tired and gave in to her dad. He hoisted her up in his arms and let her snuggle against his chest, still sniffling from her full-blown tantrum. Tracy turned to Jill and held out her arms. Jill wasn't sure what to do.

After glancing at Ed, who nodded, Jill reached out and lifted Tracy onto her lap. Her heart warmed a little as the girl rested her head on her shoulder. This was a nice feeling. She sighed.

Finally Ed motioned for her to follow him out the door. "Well, I s'pose it's time to head on home for nap time. Ready?"

Jill nodded. "Tracy, honey, would you mind walking? I need to carry my tray over to the trash can."

Tracy scrambled down, but she held on to Jill's hand. With her other hand Jill discarded her wrappers and stuffed her tray in the slot. Then she walked Tracy out to the truck where she helped her into the car seat.

She couldn't avoid noticing the curious glances in their direction—from the beginning of the tantrum until now. Everyone probably thought she was part of the family. Ed started the truck without saying a word, so Jill settled back in her seat to regroup.

They'd gone about a mile when Ed pointed his thumb toward the backseat. "They've zonked out already."

Jill glanced over her shoulder and saw two little curly-headed girls sound asleep in their car seats. The sight of them gave her a warm, fuzzy feeling she tried to ignore.

"Sweet, huh?" Ed asked.

"Yes," she agreed. "About as sweet as I've ever seen."

"A little different from twenty minutes ago." Ed snorted. "This is what happens when they get tired. Sorry you had to experience that."

When they reached the curb in front of her house, Ed turned toward her. "I think we need to talk."

Jill looked at him, waiting, without saying anything. She watched as he collected his thoughts.

"I bet you thought I was an ogre back at the restaurant."

She shook her head. "I didn't think you were an ogre."

"It's just that. . .I want them to understand how to behave in public."

"I agree." As difficult as it had been to witness what happened, Jill really did feel that something needed to be done.

"You do?"

"Well, yes, but. . ." She shrugged. "Well, I might have given in and let them have a cookie, but you can't very well allow temper tantrums in public like that."

Ed's expression softened as he let out a deep sigh. "I'm glad you're not upset with me." He glanced down, closed his eyes for a few seconds, then looked back up at her. "Jill, I'm feeling. . ."

She tilted her head. "You're feeling what?"

"I didn't want to fall in love again, but since I've met you, well. . ." He shrugged. "Maybe I shouldn't have brought it up."

She needed to know. "Since you've met me—what?"

He looked at her tenderly then glanced away. "I'm afraid I've let down my guard and allowed myself to care too much."

Conflicting emotions collided inside her. She cared for him, too, but she wasn't sure if the timing was right to let him know. She had no idea what to say next. "Um. . .I think I need to go now."

He blinked then nodded. "Okay, I understand. See ya tomorrow, bright and early." She quickly made her way up the walk, unlocked her door, opened it, and then turned to give Ed one last look before going inside. The instant the door closed behind her, she felt an overwhelming sense of exhaustion—and, to her dismay, loneliness. She thought about her relationship with her father and regretted not being more understanding. Had he just been overwhelmed with the responsibility of a child and not known what to do? Being with the twins was giving her a different perspective.

As independent as she'd always been, Jill knew she was missing some very important things in life. One thing was easily rectified: a church home. She wasn't positive yet, but she thought she'd probably found it. The other thing wasn't quite as simple.

She sank down in a living room chair, closed her eyes, and prayed.

Dear Lord, I know I haven't always been a faithful follower, so forgive me. Jill bumbled through the things she figured she'd done wrong in the Lord's eyes, and then she asked for forgiveness. It felt awkward, but she knew the Lord understood. She finished praying, opened her eyes, and sighed.

❧

When the girls woke up from their naps, they ran into the living room where Ed sat reading his Bible. He'd been trying to put everything into perspective since meeting Jill. He knew she loved his girls, and he suspected she cared for him, as well. But that wasn't enough. He didn't want to take risks—either with his heart or with his daughters'.

"Daddy, where's Jill?" Tracy asked.

"I'm not sure where she is right this minute, honey, but we dropped her off at her house a couple of hours ago."

"Can we go get her again?" Stacy said.

Ed chuckled. "No, I don't think that's such a good idea."

Tracy planted her fist on her hip and tilted her head. "And why not?"

"We don't need to smother her," he said.

"I don't want to smother her," Tracy said. "I just want her to come over."

"We need to let her have some breathing room, girls. Some space. Jill isn't used to having people with her all the time."

"She said she likes us," Stacy argued.

"She does. It's just that. . ." Ed wasn't sure what to say. He lifted both girls into his lap at the same time. "You two are growing so fast I won't be able to do this much longer." That thought saddened him.

"We ate all our lunch," Stacy said.

"But I'm still hungry," Tracy added. "Can we have a snack?"

Ed sighed. The girls were wonderful and one of the biggest blessings he'd ever had—even with the occasional angry outburst. But they sure did keep him running. "Sure, sweetie. Let's go see what we can find in the kitchen."

Since it was a couple of hours until dinnertime he fixed them each a piece of fruit, a few graham crackers, and a glass of milk. They sat at the table in booster seats while he pulled something from the freezer to thaw in the microwave.

"Can we call Jill and ask her to come over for dinner?" Tracy persisted.

"Not tonight," Ed said firmly.

"Okay, when?" Stacy asked.

It was obvious the girls weren't going to give up, so he thought for a moment. "I'm not sure that's such a good idea, girls. Jill is a very busy woman."

"Too busy for us?" Tracy asked.

What could Ed say to that? He finally said, "I can ask if she wants to go out to dinner with us one night this week."

"I want to eat here," Stacy said. "You're the bestest cook."

"I don't know about that," Ed said, "but I appreciate the compliment."

After their snack the girls ran to their room to play with some of the things Jill had given them. As he started preparing dinner, Ed thought about how he'd invite Jill to come over.

The next morning he arrived at the shop early, thinking he'd be there and finished with most of his paperwork before Jill arrived. But she'd already unlocked the front door.

"What brought you in at such an early hour?" he asked.

He sensed an emotional distance as she shrugged without looking him in the eye. "I have stuff to do."

"Oh," he said. He started to head back to his office when he remembered his promise to Stacy and Tracy. "The girls wanted me to ask you over for dinner one night this week. How about Wednesday?"

Jill quickly looked up, but she didn't say anything.

"If Tuesday is better, we can do it then. Or even Thursday. The girls really want you to. This was their idea."

She chewed on her bottom lip for a second, sighed, then nodded. "I guess Wednesday would be okay. Want me to bring something? Remember—I'm supposed to be cooking all those dinners for you and Matt, and I've only done it a couple of times."

"There'll be plenty of time for that," he said. He felt relief mixed with a little guilt. He knew mentioning the girls was a dirty tactic, but he really wanted her to come over. "It's just that the girls. . .well, you know."

"Okay, so tell me when you want me there."

The next two days passed by slowly. Each night the girls talked about all the things they wanted to show Jill when she came over. Ed imagined himself being invisible while Jill continued to charm his daughters. The amazing thing was, it didn't sound so bad. He even found himself smiling a time or two.

On Wednesday night Jill arrived at the door with a bottle of soda and a box of cookies. Ed made a quick decision before the girls saw her.

"Either the soda or the cookies. Not both."

"Huh?" Jill asked.

"Too much sugar for a couple of little girls to consume at this time of day."

She sighed as she reached over and set the soda down on the side of his porch. "Okay, you're the boss."

Several times that night Ed had to be firm with the girls, including when they needed to take their baths. As he left the room to go and run their bathwater, he felt Jill's studious gaze on him.

After their baths the girls ran into the living room to give Jill a big hug and kiss good night.

"Thank you for dinner, Ed," she said, standing. She leaned over and placed her hands on the girls' shoulders. "And I loved having dinner with you two."

Tracy chose that moment to look up at Jill. "Read us a bedtime story, Jill."

eleven

How could Jill say no to such a sweet little cherub? She glanced at Ed, who nodded, before looking back down at Tracy. "Sure, sweetie. What book do you want me to read?"

"C'mon—I'll show you all our books."

Jill let the girls pull her toward their room where she noticed the perfect neatness of the house along the way. Was there anything Ed didn't organize? She shuddered as memories of her father flashed through her mind. Then she shook off the thoughts as she remembered Ed was nothing like her father. If her father had a fraction of Ed's good qualities, like his gentle spirit and ability to listen, his other traits wouldn't have seemed so bad.

She walked into the girls' bedroom and looked around at how organized it was. Even the books were in order, according to author's last name. "We like this one," Tracy said as she pulled a thick children's Bible storybook from the shelf.

Jill chuckled nervously. "I don't have time to read that whole thing tonight."

The girls giggled. "Not the whole book, silly. Just one story."

"Oh," Jill said, smiling. "That would be just fine, then."

It took them at least ten minutes and a stern face from Ed for them to pick a story for her to read. After the story, they managed to get a glass of water each from their dad. Then they folded their little hands under their chins and took turns saying their prayers. Jill left a piece of her heart in the girls' room as she stood and walked out.

"Thanks," Ed said as they reached the front door. "That meant a lot to the girls."

Jill nodded. "It meant a lot to me, too."

"Look, Jill—there's something we need to talk about." Ed's voice cracked on his last couple of words.

"What?"

"The girls really love you, but we need to be careful not to let them get too attached to you."

Jill suddenly felt sick to her stomach. "What are you saying, Ed?"

His jaw tightened, and a serious look spread over his face. He shook his head. "The girls are starting to want more from you than just friendship."

"And what do *you* want, Ed?"

"I'm not sure it matters what I want. You know how difficult things have been for the girls."

"And for you."

He looked at her then nodded. "Yes, and for me, too. I can't deny I'm attracted to you. . . ." Her heart hammered as he paused and looked at her. "But we're so different."

She shrugged and tried to pretend she wasn't fazed. "Maybe we're not as different as you think." Now she was the one wanting more from him, but he obviously wasn't ready.

"Come on, Jill—admit that my girls can be a handful."

She sighed as she tried to find a tactful way to respond. "I know it must be hard."

They gazed into each other's eyes for several seconds before he shook his head. "We need to be careful with our relationship, or the girls will be in too deep emotionally. I don't want to destroy their spirits."

Jill looked down and swallowed deeply. "I understand."

"You're always welcome to come to church with us."

"Good night, Ed," she whispered, backing toward the door. "And thank you for everything."

He smiled. "Thanks for coming. The girls. . .and I. . .enjoyed having you."

Jill darted out the door and had to force herself to walk calmly to her car. She managed to make it home before her wobbly knees gave out on her. As she sank down into the chair, she admonished herself for letting down her guard and allowing herself to fall so deeply in love with Ed. . .and his girls.

While she was getting ready for bed, she thought about the parallels between her father and Ed, as well as the differences. Everything Ed said or did had a reason, even if she didn't agree with it. And he didn't seem to mind sharing that reason with his girls. They didn't always accept it at first, but they seemed to come around without holding a grudge.

Jill knew her grudges ran deep, and this was wrong. Her father had never given her any reasons for some of his random punishment disguised as discipline, but Ed was always clear with his daughters. With her father it was always "his way or the highway"—no questions allowed.

Granted, Ed still needed to lighten up a little. And she sensed the twins needed a little less regimen in their lives by the way their eyes lit up when they saw her. Or maybe they just liked being with her. They were thrilled to explore her shop and rummage through boxes of miscellaneous stuff. It wasn't what was in the box that excited them. It was more the unknown. The mystery. The surprise. Something Ed seemed to avoid. But he was getting better. Now he needed to allow himself to let go in a relationship with her.

With a deep sigh, Jill realized she couldn't change anything. She wanted him to love her, but she couldn't force it. She also couldn't change the fact that he was a regimented neatnik and she was a loosey-goosey slob who was happy with messy hair and her things in disarray.

Lord, thank You for making things clear to me. I don't understand all of it yet, but with Your help I'm working on it.

Jill lay in bed mulling over everything. She had no doubt Ed loved his daughters with all his heart. And he clearly hadn't broken their spirits based on their unadulterated excitement over the smallest things.

The next several days felt strange. Ed stopped by the warehouse, but he didn't spend much time there. Sometimes the girls were with him, and other times they weren't.

The following Sunday Jill went to church alone and sat with Jennifer. She saw Ed briefly, but after the services were over he'd disappeared. She went home and frantically cleaned the house, and then she fell asleep exhausted.

Early the next morning she was awakened by the phone ringing. She stumbled out of bed to answer it.

"Hey, this is Jennifer. Sorry I woke you, but I wanted to catch you before you left for the day."

"That's okay," Jill mumbled. "I needed to get up anyway. What's up?"

"Ed said he's waiting for a call from Ray. He thinks you'll be moving back to your place this weekend, so I wanted to find out when you wanted to get started."

Hmm. This was the first Jill had heard of it. "Um, I'm not sure," she said. "Can I get back to you on that?"

"I was hoping you'd know, but that's okay. I'm leaving town for a few days and won't be back until late Thursday." She paused. "Tell you what. Why don't you call and leave a message on my voice mail? I would tell you to call my cell phone, but I'm not sure I'll get service where I'm going."

"Okay, I'll do that," Jill replied.

"When I get back I'll show you some pictures. Brian and I are going on a very short cruise that's long overdue. We fly out of Atlanta tomorrow. We never had a honeymoon, unless you consider a day at Six Flags and a late dinner at the Big Chicken in Marietta romantic."

Jill laughed. "It sounds good, but I know what you mean about needing to get away for a real honeymoon."

"That's why we decided on a cruise. All the temptations from home won't be there."

"A cruise sounds nice," Jill said, holding back any feelings of jealousy. "Have fun."

"Trust me," Jennifer said with a lilt in her voice, "we will. I've heard there's so much to do on those ships that we'll need a vacation when we get back."

Jill set the phone down and lowered herself into the closest chair. *A cruise. How nice. And how absolutely wonderful Jennifer can spend the rest of her life with such a fantastic Christian man.*

Jill was truly happy for her friend but sad she'd probably never find a man with whom she could share her own life.

Ed wasn't around all day. She stayed busy waiting on customers. The next day was more of the same.

The Bible study group had decided to meet on Tuesday. She was hesitant about going. But after she got home and listened to a couple of messages from her new church friends, she figured she might as well go. At least they cared enough to call. Besides, her faith was growing in importance in her life.

The first thing people asked was, "How's Ed?" or "Where is Ed?" She was as polite as she could be when she told them she had no idea. Just as politely they nodded, then changed the subject and asked how business was. She could only guess what they were thinking.

During the fellowship time before the study, she noticed people chatting in whispers until Ed arrived. They turned and looked at him, then grew quiet. He didn't seem to notice.

The Bible study was short, but Jill was glad she'd gone. It gave her something to think about until the next time the group met.

Before leaving, Jonathan, the study leader, announced they were meeting at the Peachtree Grill on Friday night. He said he'd get there early to reserve a table and wanted to know how many could come. Jill managed to glance in Ed's direction and caught him looking at her. He smiled but didn't attempt to come over and talk to her. She felt a knot forming in her stomach. She wished things were different.

Later that night, as she was getting ready for bed, the phone rang. It was Jonathan.

"Hey, Jill, you didn't put your name down for Friday night. You're going, aren't you?"

"I'm not sure. Friday and Saturday are both big days at the shop, and. . ."

When she didn't finish her sentence, Jonathan helped her out. "It won't be a late night, I promise. We're eating at seven, and we should be out of there by nine. Why don't you go? I think you'd enjoy it."

What could she say? "I'm sure I would. Okay, put me down."

"Great! See you then."

Jill wondered if Ed would be there and what she'd say if he was. But the more she thought about it, the more she realized it didn't matter. Her friendship with Ed wouldn't change. . .or at least it shouldn't.

The next morning Ed was in his office behind the shop

when she arrived. He lifted his hand and waved but continued working. Jill felt disconcerted, but she went through all the motions of opening her shop.

❧

Ed wanted more than anything to approach Jill and ask how she was doing. If he did, he knew he would be drawn into the depths of her gorgeous, warm brown eyes. Her smile brightened his day and made him want to follow her around the shop. And when he was close enough, it took every ounce of self-restraint not to reach out and tuck her hair behind her ear. None of the physical attraction would have affected him so deeply if it hadn't been for his falling in love with who she was as a person. Yes, he finally admitted to himself that he was in love with Jill—in spite of her quirky ways. Or perhaps because of them—he wasn't sure. Whatever the case, he needed to take a step back because his daughters needed stability, and he didn't want to take any chances.

The girls had been asking about Jill, and he'd managed to change the subject by being vague. He told them she was busy with her shop and that he'd bring them to see her whenever things lightened up.

He finished filling in the paperwork for the next step of his development, but he felt fidgety. He did what he usually did when he felt this way—he went out to his shop, grabbed some scrap wood, and started working with it. He decided to build the girls a dollhouse; they'd been asking for one, and this would be the perfect time to do it.

As he sawed, he thought about the phone call he'd received the night before. Jonathan wanted him to go to the dinner party on Friday night. Ed rarely went to those things, but he gave in. He thought he might get to see Jill. He knew that probably wasn't good for him, but he missed her. For the past couple of days he'd been avoiding her until he couldn't stand it anymore.

He was cutting the last of the wood to build the sides of the dollhouse when the phone in his office rang. It was Ray, the exterminator.

"Good news," Ray said. "We finished everything. The tent comes off tomorrow as planned."

"That's really good news," Ed said with a heavy heart. "Thanks. I'll tell Jill."

"I'll call her if you want me to."

"No." Ed glanced up in time to see Jill coming from behind her counter to help a customer who'd just walked in. "She's in her shop right now. After she finishes with this customer, I'll let her know."

Ed thought that was the end of the conversation, but Ray apparently thought otherwise. "I know you're not asking for advice, Ed, but I'm gonna give it to you anyway. This girl is special. You need to hang on to her."

"I don't know what you're talking about, Ray." Ed shifted his weight to the other foot.

Ray chuckled. "Oh, I think you know, buddy. She's been coming to church regularly, and from what I can tell she loves the Lord. She's a sweet woman, and you show all the signs of being smitten. That's as good a start as any of us get."

Ed swallowed hard. "Thanks for the advice, Ray. I'll think about it."

After Jill was finished with her customer, Ed approached her. "Ray just called. The extermination is finished." He tried to keep his voice on an even keel, but he knew it was shaky. The mere thought of not having an excuse to see Jill every day depressed him.

Jill glanced down then looked at him. "Good. Thanks. I'll see about moving back."

"I'll call everyone to help," Ed said. "We'll get most of it done this weekend."

Jill started to say something, but another group of customers walked in. "We can talk about it later," she said as she edged toward her customers.

Later never came. The shop stayed busy for the remainder of the day, and Ed had errands to run. Not only was Jill about to move back to her own place, he was very close to starting his new development, meaning he'd hardly have time to see her.

As always, the girls greeted him the minute he walked in the door. Emma came around the corner from the kitchen, grinning. "How's Jill?" she asked.

He shrugged. "Fine, I guess. Oh, by the way, we're moving her back into her shop this weekend. Would you mind calling a few people to let them know?"

"Can we help, Daddy?" Stacy asked.

Ed turned around to see his little girls staring up at him with hands clasped beneath their chins. His heart twitched. "Of course you can, but you have to do exactly what I tell you to do."

They jumped up and down, squealing with delight. Ed chuckled and turned to Emma.

"They'll have a good time helping," Emma said, "but I'll be there, just in case you need me to help out with them."

Emma truly was a blessing. Ever since she and George had arrived, the entire church experience was not only a great place to be fed spiritually, but it had also become a true community. Their giving nature had filtered down to the congregation, and everyone had started pitching in to serve.

"Another thing, Ed. . . ," Emma continued. "If you need someone to watch the girls Friday night, I'm available."

Ed couldn't help but smile. "You're an angel, Emma."

"No, I'm just a very good friend who cares about you. I want you to get out more and have a good time. You work hard." She moved toward the door. "What time do you want me here?"

They made arrangements; then she left. The girls were still excited, but they'd calmed down enough for dinner, which Emma had started cooking.

"This is the best b'sketti I ever had," Tracy said as she twisted her fork around a strand of noodles. "Jill would like it, too."

"I'm sure she would."

Ed needed to find another measure for both his daughters and himself. They couldn't keep thinking about everything in relation to what Jill would like.

After the girls ate, he did his regular evening routine with them, running their bathwater and reading a story once they were in their pajamas. The girls were being too well-behaved, though, which left him no doubt they were up to something.

The rest of Ed's week was extremely busy, organizing Jill's move, and then finishing the paperwork on his new development. He wanted to tell Jill about it, but her shop was so crowded all the time that he didn't have much of a chance. It was certainly obvious she'd hit on something that had taken off.

He still felt out of sorts. Everything on the surface of his life looked excellent. He had two very happy, healthy daughters. He loved everything about his church, and his faith in the Lord was growing. And Jill was doing well, so he didn't have to worry about her anymore. Nevertheless, something was bothering him.

By Friday afternoon Ed was ready for a little rest. Dinner with the church group would be the perfect ending to his productive week.

Jennifer called his cell phone as he was about to leave the warehouse. "I've been trying to get in touch with Jill," she said. "Is she there?"

Ed leaned over and saw that the lights in the shop were off. "Doesn't look like it."

"She's not at home, either."

A touch of concern flickered through Ed. "Is something wrong?"

Jennifer laughed. "No, I just had a few things I needed to ask about. We've been trying to find an easier way to haul all that glass tomorrow."

Ed wandered toward the shop and took a long look around. "Seems she has everything packed in boxes—at least all the small stuff."

"Yeah, I know. I was there helping her this afternoon."

"Don't worry about the glass. We'll get it moved just fine. Oh, how was the cruise?" Ed asked, hoping to change the subject.

"It was better than I ever expected. Brian and I were talking about what a great honeymoon it would make."

Ed practically ran into the wall in front of him. "I'm sure. Look—I have some stuff to do, so I'll see you later."

"If you see Jill, tell her to give me a call. I left messages, but she doesn't always check her voice mail."

"Will do," Ed said as he clicked the END button on his phone.

Not checking voice mail was another characteristic of Jill's nature. He checked his at least three or four times a day. What if she missed something important?

Ed headed home where the girls were playing with the same old boxes of toys Jill had given them when they first met. He'd come to accept the fact that it wasn't all junk.

Emma handed him his mail as he passed her. "Mrs. Cooper called and said it'll be a few more weeks before she can come back."

Ed's insides knotted. "Oh, that's just great. In the meantime, what am I supposed to do?"

"That's what I'm here for." Emma narrowed her eyes. "You need to learn to relax, Ed, or you'll have a heart attack."

Ed rubbed the back of his neck. "Sorry I took it out on you. It's just that I've got so much going on, I don't know what to do."

"Well, first of all, prayer helps."

"Yeah," he agreed. "I do plenty of that."

"You also need to accept the blessings from the Lord." Emma paused before continuing. "He's brought a bunch of people into your life, and we're all willing to help."

"And I certainly appreciate it," Ed said with a half smile. "But I don't want to overdo it with the child care."

"We consider your girls our blessing," she said. "So stop worrying. Have you ever thought that maybe your biggest problem might be your too-high expectations rather than too much to do?"

Ed opened his mouth but decided it was better not to argue and clamped it shut. Emma studied him for another second before he started to leave.

On his way out the door, he turned to Emma. "I won't be too late. I really apprec—"

She smiled. "I know, Ed. And I love being here with the girls. Have a great time."

"Have fun, Daddy," Stacy said. "Tell Jill to come see us."

"I will," he replied. "That is, if I see her."

All the way to the restaurant he thought about how his girls had become attached to Jill. It was painfully obvious they needed a woman in their lives—and not just a babysitter. And being honest with himself, Ed realized Jill had awakened something inside him that brightened the world around him. A couple of times he'd actually entertained the thought of giving in to his attraction to Jill to see where things could go for them. But reality always kicked in when their differences jumped in the way. Marcy had been a little messy, but Jill made her look like Mrs. Clean. Even without that issue, though, he couldn't forget how devastated the girls would be if things didn't work out and Jill turned her back on them.

He parked his car and was about to open the door when he noticed a familiar figure walking toward him. He glanced up in time to see Jill, who had just spotted him, nearly trip over the curb.

twelve

"Whoa there," Ed said, running up to her. "You okay?"

She nodded. "Yes, I just wasn't watching. Sorry I'm so late."

Ed glanced at his watch. "You're not late. In fact, we're both right on time."

Jill tilted her head to one side. "But I thought. . .I was supposed to be here fifteen minutes ago." She frowned then shook her head. "Never mind. Let's just go inside, okay?"

As soon as they walked in and saw the group seated at the table, with two empty chairs beside each other, Ed's suspicions were confirmed. He'd been told when to get there, and knowing he was always punctual, everyone else had arrived early. Based on what Jill said, they must have wanted her there waiting for him—or they figured she'd be late.

Rather than make a fuss, Ed accepted that it was a setup with Jill. She looked as uncomfortable as he was.

The entire two hours were spent being on show for the rest of the people in the group. Everyone obviously wanted him and Jill to get together. He wanted it, too, and he had missed her so much he was finally willing to take a risk.

As soon as she finished her dinner, Jill grabbed her purse. "Sorry, but I have to run. I have an early morning tomorrow with the move and all."

It was dark outside by then. Ed stood. "I'll walk you to your car."

"You don't have to," Jill said quickly.

"He's being a gentleman," Jennifer whispered.

Jill looked at her friend then at Ed. "Okay," she told him.

Jill's discomfort ripped at Ed's heart. Once they reached her car, he made sure she was safely inside. She rolled down her window. "Thanks, Ed. I'll see you tomorrow, okay?"

"You know I wasn't in on this setup, don't you?" he said.

She paused then nodded. "Yes, of course."

He couldn't think of a way to mention how he felt, so he said, "Drive safely. I'll see you bright and early along with the rest of those clowns." He took a step back. "Stacy and Tracy are coming, but Emma will take them home if they start acting up."

Jill smiled. His heart did a double-loopy thing.

"G'night," she whispered. He waved then turned and walked away.

&

He must have been brushing me off, Jill thought. He made such an issue of not being in on the setup. Deep down she'd hoped he'd set it up himself. She loved everything about him—including his incredible sense of responsibility. Through Ed she'd learned that discipline was a good thing if done right. Not only did she love his girls, but she was also in love with everything about Ed—from his desire to fix her life to the Christian kindness he showed everyone in his path. Jill had never met a man with such integrity.

She tossed and turned all night, mulling over his reaction to what the group had tried to do. Even though it was meddlesome, she thought it was sweet that they cared enough to go to that much trouble.

When morning finally arrived, Jill dressed in jeans and her favorite T-shirt from the bank. She took a couple of sips of coffee before heading out. It was unseasonably warm, but in north Georgia that wasn't unusual. It could be snowing one day and short-sleeve weather the next.

The parking lot at the warehouse was already filled with

pickup trucks and SUVs. Ed had let them in, but no one had started loading yet. The second she arrived, a couple of the men approached her.

"We'd like to take the big stuff over first while y'all pack the smaller boxes," one of them said.

Jennifer's husband, Brian, pointed toward a white truck with the tailgate down. "How about the desk first?"

"Sure," Jill replied. "Whatever you think is best."

Three hours later Jill was back in her own shop with the desk in place. She'd shown them which boxes needed to go first; then Ed suggested she go to the shop to supervise unloading. By the end of the day everything was at the shop, and all the big pieces were in place. Ed's daughters had helped unpack a couple of boxes, but they lost interest and begged to go home. Before they left with Emma, they ran up to Jill for a hug.

She noticed Ed watching, but he quickly turned away when their gazes met. The rest of the afternoon went by in a flash.

"This is simply amazing," Jill said as she took a long look around.

"Yeah, we have a good group," Brian said. "If you need anything else, just give us a holler."

After a few minutes the place had cleared out, with the exception of Ed and Jill. "Want me to stick around a little longer?" he asked.

"No, thanks. I have everything under control," she replied. *Except my heart, but that's not open for discussion.*

"Then I need to get home to the girls. I'll see you in church tomorrow."

After he left, Jill blew out a deep breath. The emotional roller coaster she'd been on since she'd met Ed had left her exhausted even more than the physical move. Now maybe she'd have some time to think and figure out how to manage her personal life. With the shop in place and plenty of regular customers, she felt more confident she'd be able to make a living.

After putting the last of the glass knickknacks on the shelves, Jill locked the door and sat in an old wooden rocker for some quiet time. She bowed her head in prayer and focused on all she had to be thankful for. Closure with Ed was on her mind, but she didn't know where to begin with that prayer.

She went to church the next morning, but she saw the gleam in some eyes as people looked back and forth between her and Ed. So she scooted out of there as quickly as she could without being rude.

Over the next couple of weeks, Ed stopped in when he could to finish his work. He updated her on the progress of his development and how busy it was keeping him. After he had completed the last of the projects, Jill asked about the girls.

"Emma's been watching them," he said. "Mrs. Cooper's coming back next week, so things should be pretty much back to the way they were."

"Oh," Jill said. "That's nice." She couldn't even force a smile.

Ed had taken a step back, but he stopped. "What are you thinking, Jill?"

She shrugged. "I don't know. I miss seeing them. I sort of got attached, you know?"

He chuckled. "Yeah, I know what you're saying. I'm kind of attached to them myself."

She managed to grin. "Why don't you bring them by sometime so I can see them?"

His face lit up. "They'd like that," he said. "But I know you're busy."

She watched as Ed drew closer. "I'm never too busy for your daughters, Ed. I really enjoy being around them."

He looked down at his feet. "Well, I guess I'd better run," he finally said. "See ya."

Suddenly she knew she couldn't let him go that easily. "Wait, Ed."

He turned to face her, one eyebrow lifted. "Do you need something?"

She nodded slowly. "We need to talk."

"Talk?"

He sure wasn't making this easy for her. "Yes. About us. I, uh. . ."

Ed paused then closed the gap between them. "What's on your mind?"

Jill swallowed. She knew exactly what she wanted to say, but it was risky. Until now she'd been willing to take risks, but this was different. This wasn't just about money or a business. This dealt with her heart.

He reached for both of her hands and squeezed them. "It must be important for you to hold back like this. Are you afraid of something?"

She nodded. "Yes, very."

"You don't have to be. This is me. Ed. I'm your friend, remember?"

Finally she sucked in a breath. "That's part of the problem."

He blinked. "Huh?"

"Before I met you, I thought I knew exactly what I wanted; then you came along with your girls. You were there to help, and that confused me because I didn't understand why you were so eager to help someone who obviously couldn't pay you. Now I do."

He smiled. "You've come a long way, Jill, but then so have I. I think we understand each other better now."

"I'm not so sure. After watching you in action, fixing my shop and being a father—a wonderful father—I see things differently now. Faith in Christ is personal, but it's also a way of life."

Now his smile spread across his face, and his eyes even crinkled. "I see a few things differently now, too. You're a wonderful, kindhearted, responsible woman who's been badly hurt. Let's give our thoughts and feelings some time to simmer; then perhaps we can talk more later."

Before she'd gotten to know Ed, that kind of talk would have made her crazy, but his slower, methodical process made sense to her now. She was willing to wait until they were both ready to talk more.

He pulled her close, tilted her face up, and kissed her on the tip of her nose. Then he let go of her and slowly backed away. "I'll check on you every now and then. Call if you need me."

After he left, Jill immersed herself in organizing things in the shop. She felt a combination of emotions—from elation to concern. When she felt worry tugging at her heart, she went to the Lord in prayer.

The next week was busier than ever for Jill. Now that she had more capital to work with from early sales and she knew what her clientele wanted, she was able to carry a higher quality of antiques. Ed had stopped by periodically and made comments about the changes. The fact that he noticed warmed her heart even more.

"I know this seems like a random thought, but would you like to join the girls and me for dinner on Friday night?" Ed asked one afternoon when he'd stopped by on his way to the courthouse to take care of business on his development.

Jill wanted more than anything to be with him and the girls, but her feelings for Ed had intensified even more now that she only saw him on Sundays and once in a while when he had time to stop by the shop. "I don't know," she said. She didn't want to be a random thought.

"The girls wanted me to ask you," he said. "What should I tell them?"

This put a different light on things. She didn't like disappointing Stacy and Tracy. "The girls put you up to this?"

He nodded. "They miss you."

"*They* miss me?"

He paused, grinned, and added, "I miss you, too. Please say yes."

How could she turn down such an offer? "Okay, I'll be glad to go."

"Since you close at six we can pick you up at six thirty at your house, if that's okay with you."

She nodded. "That'll be just fine."

The rest of the week Jill kept hoping Ed would stop by again, but he didn't.

On Friday, before going to the shop, Jill put out some clothes to change into after work. Then she headed for the shop, hoping for a busy day so it would go by quickly. Her wish came true. She had a steady stream of customers throughout the day.

She couldn't seem to get out of there fast enough. As soon as she could, she flipped the sign to CLOSED, then dashed to her car. Ed was always on time, so she drove home, ran inside, and changed. A glance at the clock in her living room let her know she'd barely made it with one minute to spare. She sat on the edge of the sofa to kill the minute she had, but six thirty came and went, and still no Ed. Her nerves almost got the best of her when he was ten minutes late. She'd just stood to call his cell phone when the doorbell rang. It was Tracy.

"Daddy and Stacy are in the car waiting," she said. "They made me come get you cuz I'm the one who made us late. Stacy unbuckled me as soon as Daddy stopped the car. All Daddy had to do was open the door for me."

Jill smiled at the worry lines etched on the little girl's face. "That's okay, honey. I'm usually the one who's late, so it's no big deal."

"I know that. Daddy told me you're always late, and that's why we never take you with us."

Suddenly Jill felt as if she'd hit a brick wall. "Your daddy told you that?"

Tracy nodded. "But that's okay. Stacy and I still love you. And we think Daddy does, too, because he's so happy you're going out to eat with us."

Now Jill had no idea what to think as she walked out to Ed's truck with Tracy. Stacy's little face was pressed against the window.

"Sorry we're late," Ed said as he climbed out and helped her and Tracy into the truck.

Jill offered a half smile. "Don't worry about it."

Throughout the meal Jill chatted with the girls about everything that was going on in their lives. Stacy told her about Sunday school, and Tracy told her about the dollhouse her daddy had made for the dolls she'd given them. Jill avoided looking at Ed. Out of the corner of her eye she saw him watching her, a pained expression on his face.

After dinner the girls wanted to play in the arcade next door. Ed asked Jill if that was okay, and she nodded.

"Is something bothering you, Jill?" Ed asked the minute they were alone.

She had to ask him. "Yes," she finally said. "Did you tell Tracy you didn't want to take me with you anywhere because I'm always late?"

Ed's eyes widened. "No, but I guess I can imagine where she got the idea. One time when they asked if we could take you to church I said no, that we would be late if we came to pick you up, especially if you didn't know we were coming."

Jill let out her breath and smiled then. She was glad she had asked.

They were there for a half hour when Stacy started whining

and stamping her feet. When Ed reprimanded her, Jill looked away.

Finally, after Ed had told Stacy not to do something and she did it anyway, he took both girls by the hand and said it was time to leave. Stacy continued whining and talking back, but Ed stayed firm. It was evident to Jill that the girls were tired.

Ed helped Stacy into the truck while Jill buckled Tracy into her car seat. By the time they arrived at Jill's house, both girls were sound asleep.

He reached out and took her hand. "Thanks for going out with us. I'm sorry about the girls' behavior."

"I totally understand."

He tilted his head and looked at her before a grin spread across his face. "Yes, I think you really do understand."

"Thanks for the great evening, Ed. Tell the girls I enjoyed being with them, and I hope to see them again soon."

Jill sat and studied him for a moment before he reached out and touched her cheek. "I'll call you, okay?"

She nodded before she let herself out and headed up the sidewalk to her house. She'd had fun until the temper tantrum, but even that didn't take away from the pleasure of being with Ed and the girls.

Saturday was busy at the shop, which kept her from thinking about Ed too much. But Sunday was different. Each time she was near Ed, she felt flustered and giddy, which made her uncomfortable around their friends.

Jennifer stopped by the shop the next morning. "Okay, girl, what's going on between you and Ed?"

Jill hadn't come out and said anything about her feelings to anyone, and she preferred not to now. But she didn't want to brush Jennifer off.

"I understand what you all are trying to do," she said, "but there are some things Ed and I need to work out."

"Like what?"

"Well, for one, we're really different."

"So?" Jennifer said. "Brian and I are different, but that's what makes our relationship so interesting."

"Yeah, but he didn't have kids when you met him."

Jennifer frowned. "But I thought you loved Ed's girls."

"I do, but. . ." Jill tried to find the right words, but finally lifted her hands in surrender. "Oh, never mind. It's useless to try to explain."

Jennifer gazed at her a moment then nodded. "I think I have a pretty good idea of what's going on. It's obvious to the rest of us that you and Ed are crazy about each other, and it seems like a no-brainer to us. But you both have conflicting issues."

"Yeah," Jill said with a snicker. "That's an understatement."

"What neither of you seems to realize is that you don't have to agree on everything. If people only got together with other people who agreed with them, no one would ever get married."

"Some of our differences are pretty major," Jill replied.

Jennifer sighed then glanced at her watch. "I have to run now. I'm sorry." She smiled. "Just think about what I said, okay?"

"Sure. But don't get your hopes up."

For the rest of the day Jill thought about Jennifer's comments. They weighed so heavily on her that she couldn't focus on business. Her distraction must have shown because one of her regular customers, Mrs. Brighton, asked her if she was having "man problems," as she put it.

"I was always out of sorts when Henry and I had an argument," she said. Then she offered a sly grin and wiggled her eyebrows. "But things always got better, and we more than made up for whatever we were arguing about. That man was the best kisser in the whole world."

Jill smiled at the older woman. "That's sweet."

Mrs. Brighton blushed. "Don't let petty differences ruin your day. Life's too short for that. Might as well start kissing and making up right away, sweetie. That's the whole point of the argument, anyway."

Everyone seemed concerned about her. Even Matt stopped by to ask if she was okay.

"I'm fine, but I'd be better if you'd let me finish cooking all those meals to pay you back."

"It's better to spread it out," he said, chuckling. "Unless you want to get it over with."

"No, that's okay. We can do it over time. I just don't want you to think I've forgotten about it."

The next morning when she arrived at the shop, Ed was sitting on the front porch waiting for her, holding a paper bag. "I brought bagels," he said. "Raisin bagels with extra cream cheese, the way you like them."

"Thanks," Jill said as she unlocked the door to the shop. "Come on in."

He followed her inside and helped her turn on the lights. Finally, once everything was ready for opening, Ed walked up to Jill and took her hand. "I've been wondering if maybe we could start over."

"Start over?"

He nodded. "Yeah, like maybe go out on a date and get to know each other all over again."

"Has everyone been talking to you, too?"

Ed tilted his head back and laughed. "Of course they have. And I'm okay with that. How about you?"

She shrugged. "People have said stuff." She turned and headed toward the counter where Ed had left the bagels.

"Well? How do you feel about it?" he asked.

"About what?"

"Maybe we could get together and see how things go." He glanced down then looked up at her, waiting for her answer.

Her heart thudded. "That would be nice."

"Let's go somewhere Saturday evening. I promised the girls I'd take them out for tacos on Friday, but I'm free Saturday."

"Saturday's fine," Jill replied.

"Okay, I'll pick you up at seven. Gotta run. I have a ton of work to do on the new development tomorrow."

"How's the project coming?"

He shrugged. "I've had more glitches than I'm used to, but I think we're on track now."

After he left, Jill thought about her date with Ed. It was weird how he'd just stopped by like that. She had no delusions that anything would be different, but she couldn't flat out turn him down when he'd met her with her favorite bagels—with extra cream cheese, at that.

She had a banner sales week, so by the time Saturday night arrived she was exhausted but in a wonderful mood. Ed commented on her good mood when he picked her up.

"Want to go to a movie?" he asked.

"That's fine. Is there something you'd like to see?"

He shook his head. "No, I can't think of anything. I don't even know why I suggested it. It's hard to talk in a movie. We should probably do something different."

"How about bowling?"

Ed chuckled. "Do you like to bowl?"

She smiled back at him. "I don't know. I've never done it, but I'm willing to give it a try. I guess it's about time I tried something new." This was a major turning point for her, and she wanted him to know it, too.

With a smile he took her by the hand and led her to his truck. "After you catch on to the technique, I have a feeling you'll be an excellent bowler."

At first Jill rolled a few gutter balls at the bowling alley, but she couldn't remember ever having so much fun. She felt giddy and lighthearted for the first time since she was a little girl.

"See?" he said as they pulled out of the parking lot. "You caught on fast."

"That's because you're a good teacher."

"So are you," he said softly.

Her eyes widened. "Huh? I've never taught you anything," she said, then added, "Have I?"

He pulled into the parking lot of a convenience store, then turned to her. "Since I've known you, you've taught me to lighten up. You've shown me how to be spontaneous. You've brought beauty and joy into my life, Jill."

Tears stung the backs of Jill's eyes as she took in everything he was saying. "Thank you," she whispered.

"No." He leaned over and dropped a soft kiss on her lips. "Thank you."

Without another word he pulled out of the parking lot and drove her home. He walked her to her door and then stood and gazed at her. Jill reached up and touched her palm to his cheek. "Good night, Ed," she said softly.

Then he did the unexpected. He took her hand in his and drew her to him. Next thing she knew, his lips were gently on hers. She felt as if her heart were turning somersaults as he kissed her good night.

He released her and quickly stepped away. "Good night, Jill," he said.

Her lips still tingled from his kiss as she got ready for bed. The next morning she almost decided not to go to church. How could she face Ed after last night? That kiss meant much more to her than it could possibly have meant to him.

Then she came to her senses. She needed to go to church. That was what kept her grounded all week. So she reined in her feelings and went, but she stayed in the back and avoided contact with any of her friends. When church was over, she pretended not to see Jennifer waving to her. Instead she darted out the side door and hurried to her car before anyone could say something.

Monday morning was slower than usual. When she heard the bell on the door jingle right before noon, she looked up, expecting a customer. It was Ed and the twins. Tracy and Stacy ran to her and flung their little arms around her. She hugged them before looking up at Ed.

"They wanted to see you," he said as he strode toward her like a soldier on a mission.

Something in the way Ed was looking at her made her feel woozy inside. She couldn't pull her gaze away from his.

"Girls," he said firmly, "take your puzzles and go play in the back room while I talk to Jill for a minute."

The girls exchanged a glance then did as they were told. Once he and Jill were alone, Ed studied her for several seconds before he finally spoke. "We need to talk about this before it gets any worse."

"Talk about what?"

"You know," he replied. "Our feelings."

Jill's heart pounded. "What about our feelings?"

"I love you, and I think you love me."

Suddenly Ed's cell phone rang. "Excuse me a second, okay?"

Ed took the call while Jill went to the back room and asked the girls how they were doing. With excitement they talked over each other, telling her about everything in their lives—from their new toys to Mrs. Cooper's new grandbaby.

When Ed got off the phone, he was grimacing. "Sandra Chimensky's little girl locked herself in the bathroom, and they can't get the door open. Sandra called a locksmith, but she can't afford the fee. She knows I have the tools to take the door off the hinge. Would you mind watching the girls while I run over there and let her out?"

"Go ahead," Jill said. "We'll be fine."

Ed was gone only a few minutes when the shop became crowded. Jill took the girls back to the table and pulled out some things for them to play with. "I'll be right out there if you need me," she said.

She waited on a couple of customers before she realized how quiet it was in the back of the shop. An uneasy feeling crept over Jill as she headed back to find out what they were doing. The instant she rounded the corner, a strong sulfur smell overwhelmed her. She paused. To her surprise both girls were striking matches against a matchbox.

"No!" she hollered, running to them. "Stop! Now!"

At once Stacy looked up, her eyes wide open. When she saw Jill, her chin began to quiver. Tracy took a step back in fear.

"What do you think you're doing?" Jill cried. She'd never yelled at anyone, but these were extreme circumstances. By the time she yanked the matches from their hands and grabbed both of the girls' arms, Tracy was crying and calling for her daddy. Stacy was pouting, but she didn't cry.

"Sit down, both of you," Jill demanded, pointing her finger toward the chairs. An unfamiliar fear washed over her as she imagined the result if she hadn't caught them before it was too late. The building was old and had a wood frame. It would have gone up in flames so fast she didn't want to think what might have happened to the girls.

"Do you know how dangerous it is to play with matches?" she said firmly.

"We weren't playing with matches," Stacy said.

"Don't lie, Stacy," Jill said. "I saw you."

"She's not lying. We were trying to light these candles we found. You were busy. We didn't want to bother you," Tracy said.

"Those are for adults, not children." Jill shook her finger at both girls. "You are not allowed to touch a match again until you're grown. Do you understand?"

They both nodded.

"I know your daddy well enough to know he'd never allow you to light matches."

Stacy suddenly leaned forward and looked past her. "Daddy, Jill's yelling at us!"

Jill whirled around and saw Ed standing in the doorway, taking it all in. "How long have you been standing there?" she asked.

"Long enough to know what's going on. I got the Chimensky door open quickly and came right back." He walked over and bent over toward the girls. "Were you listening to Jill just now?"

Stacy sniffled and nodded. "She's being mean to us."

Ed rolled his eyes. "You know better than that. I've told you girls never to play with matches. Jill cares about you, and she's letting you know."

"B–but she yelled."

"I know." Ed turned to Jill and gave her the thumbs-up sign. "And I would have yelled, too, if I'd caught you lighting matches."

Tracy had stopped crying, but Stacy was sobbing now. Jill watched as Ed squatted between them with his arms around their shoulders.

"You realize this means you can't go to that movie party on Friday night, don't you?"

"But, Daddy," Stacy whimpered, "that's not fair."

Ed glanced up at Jill. When she nodded and turned to Stacy, he said, "You owe Jill an apology for misbehaving in her shop."

In the past Jill would have told him that wasn't necessary, but things were different now. She understood his need to discipline his daughters, and she knew humility was part of the training.

"Girls, I want you to know the only reason I yelled at you was because I love you," Jill said. "If anything ever happened to either of you. . ." She shuddered. "I don't even want to think about that."

Tracy stood up and came over to her. "We love you, too."

To Jill's surprise Stacy came too, and the three hugged each other. Stacy sniffled as she mumbled, "We're sorry we were bad. We won't ever do that again."

❧

Ed's heart melted as he watched this tender moment between Jill and his daughters. He could see her as part of his family. She'd appreciated his parenting methods, and he understood her softness with the girls. Not only was he deeply in love with her, but he knew she'd be a positive influence on the girls. He needed to take the girls home now, though.

"C'mon, girls. Let's give Jill a break so she can work." He looked at Jill. "I'll talk to you later, okay?" Jill nodded. He took them out to the truck and put them in their car seats.

"Daddy," Stacy said once they were on their way home, "I don't want Jill to be mad at us."

"She was upset because you were doing something really bad, something that could have hurt you," Ed said. "Jill loves you."

"Are you sure she loves us?" Tracy asked.

"I don't think she'd say anything she doesn't mean."

He looked at the girls in his rearview mirror in time to catch them exchanging a glance.

"Daddy, do you love Jill?"

"Why are you asking?"

"Since we love Jill, and she loves us back, we were thinking—." He saw Tracy hold her fingers up to her lips. Stacy stopped midsentence.

"What's going on?" he asked.

The girls giggled. "Can Jill be our mommy?"

Ed chuckled. Just what he'd thought. "Why don't we let her recover from the match incident first; then we can talk about that."

Fifteen minutes later they approached him again. "Do you think she's recovered yet?"

"Maybe."

"Can she marry us?"

Ed sighed. He couldn't keep his feelings to himself any longer. He'd already decided he wanted to marry her, but he also wanted to have a romantic proposal—alone with Jill. He didn't want to deny his daughters the pleasure they'd obviously get from his decision, though.

He looked into each expectant face and smiled. "I plan to ask her very soon."

Both girls turned to each other and squealed with delight. The girls were remarkably well behaved for the rest of the day. That night, they even got ready for bed and turned in early.

The next morning Ed was awakened by two little girls jumping on his bed. He rolled over and squinted.

"Get up, Daddy."

"What time is it?"

Stacy held out her hands and shrugged. "The big hand is on the twelve, and the little hand is on the seven."

"Let me sleep a few more minutes."

"But we have to go to work."

"Huh?"

"We want to go to work with you at Jill's shop."

"I've finished my work at Jill's shop."

"Daddy," Stacy said firmly, "we want to see Jill. So get up and let's go."

He wasn't in the mood to argue, so he swung his legs over

the side of the bed. Besides, the thought of seeing Jill sounded pretty good. "Okay, but I have to shower and get dressed first."

By the time he was dressed, both girls had their clothes on and were at the kitchen table eating cereal. Mrs. Cooper had put plastic bowls within their reach and small, pint-sized cartons of milk on the lower refrigerator shelf so they could be more self-sufficient. "We fixed you some, so sit down and eat," Stacy said, pointing to a bowl with soggy corn flakes floating around.

Fifteen minutes later they were on their way to the shop. "She might not be in yet," Ed said. "It's still early."

"She'll be there," Stacy said, pointing her finger. "See? There's her car. We called her and said it was a 'mergency."

"You what?" He'd just pulled up in front of the shop and stopped the truck. Before either girl answered they were out of their car seats and trying to get out of the door. He laughed at how they'd teamed up and unbuckled each other's seat belts. He started to hold back and not let the girls out, but at this point he knew it was useless. The second he opened the door, they were out of the truck and halfway up the sidewalk.

Jill opened the front door of the shop, and the girls ran right up to her. Ed was on their heels.

"Jill," Stacy said, "we wanna ask you something real important." She turned to Ed. "Daddy, c'mere."

Ed did as he was told. "Now what?"

"Will you be our mommy?" Tracy blurted.

"Huh?" Jill said.

Tracy rolled her eyes. "That's not how you do it, Stacy." She turned to Jill. "Will you marry our daddy?"

Jill looked as if she might fall over backward. Ed rushed to her side. "You okay, Jill?"

"I, uh," she stammered, "I don't know what to say."

The corners of his lips curled as he gave her a teasing look.

"Just answer their question."

Jill's eyes widened in disbelief.

Ed reached down, cupped her face in his hands, and whispered, "Please say yes."

epilogue

"Brush my hair, Jill," Stacy said. "I want to be pretty like you."

"You look beautiful," Jill said as she ran the brush through Stacy's curls. "How's my veil?"

She leaned toward the girls, who inspected it and nodded. "You're the prettiest bride in the whole wide world," Tracy told her.

Jill's eyes misted as she hugged her soon-to-be daughters. "And you two are the prettiest flower girls in the whole wide world."

The organ began to play. Jill stood and gently guided the twins out the door. "It's time to go down the aisle, girls."

Stacy nudged in front of Tracy. "I wanna go first."

"No, I want to go first."

"Girls," Jill said, her voice low and firm. They giggled. "You can walk together, side by side, okay?"

After the girls were halfway down the aisle, Jill had an overwhelming surge of maternal feelings. She wished her father could have been there to witness this wonderful moment. She glanced over at Jennifer, who'd taken her position right behind the twins and was about to walk toward the front of the church.

Matt extended his elbow, and she took it. "Thanks for walking me down the aisle, Matt."

"Trust me—it's an honor to bring my best buddy the woman he loves."

She giggled. As the music changed, her heart pounded with excitement and anticipation of the full life she had ahead of her.

The doors opened wide, allowing everyone in the church to see her as she made her entrance. She took her first step toward Ed, the man she loved with all her heart. "Oohs" and "aahs" echoed throughout the church.

Then suddenly the girls piped up. "Here comes our new mommy!"

A Letter To Our Readers

Dear Reader:

In order that we might better contribute to your reading enjoyment, we would appreciate your taking a few minutes to respond to the following questions. We welcome your comments and read each form and letter we receive. When completed, please return to the following:

Fiction Editor
Heartsong Presents
PO Box 719
Uhrichsville, Ohio 44683

1. Did you enjoy reading *Double Blessing* by Debby Mayne?
   ❏ Very much! I would like to see more books by this author!
   ❏ Moderately. I would have enjoyed it more if

   _____

   _____

   _____

2. Are you a member of **Heartsong Presents**? ❏ Yes ❏ No
   If no, where did you purchase this book? _____

   _____

3. How would you rate, on a scale from 1 (poor) to 5 (superior), the cover design? _____

4. On a scale from 1 (poor) to 10 (superior), please rate the following elements.

   ____ Heroine   ____ Plot
   ____ Hero   ____ Inspirational theme
   ____ Setting   ____ Secondary characters

5. These characters were special because? _____

_____

_____

6. How has this book inspired your life? _____

_____

_____

7. What settings would you like to see covered in future
   Heartsong Presents books? _____

_____

_____

8. What are some inspirational themes you would like to see
   treated in future books? _____

_____

_____

9. Would you be interested in reading other **Heartsong
   Presents** titles? ❏ Yes ❏ No

10. Please check your age range:
    ❏ Under 18   ❏ 18-24
    ❏ 25-34   ❏ 35-45
    ❏ 46-55   ❏ Over 55

Name _____

Occupation _____

Address _____

City, State, Zip _____

Virginia WEDDINGS

3 stories in 1

*T*hree single Virginia women at very different stages in life each find something missing from their lives.

Stories by author Lauralee Bliss include: *Ageless Love*, *Time Will Tell*, and *The Wish*.

Contemporary, paperback, 352 pages, 5³/₁₆" x 8"